SCi-Fi
BaBy names

D1041065

SCi-Fi
BABY NAMES

500 OUT-OF-THIS-WORLD BABY NAMES
FROM ANAKIN TO ZARDOZ

BY ROBERT SCHNAKENBERG

QUIRK BOOKS
PHILADELPHIA

Copyright © 2007 by Robert Schnakenberg

Library of Congress Cataloging in Publication Number: 2007922636

ISBN: 978-1-59474-161-6

Printed in China

Typeset in Bubbledot, House 3009, Russel Square, and TradeGothic

Designed by Doogie Horner
Illustrations by Carl Wiens

Distributed in North America by Chronicle Books
680 Second Street
San Francisco, CA 94107

10 9 8 7 6 5 4 3 2 1

Quirk Books
215 Church Street
Philadelphia, PA 19106
www.quirkbooks.com

CONTENTS

INTRODUCTION

Congratulations! If you're reading this, you're probably expecting a baby. Now what are you going to call the little bundle of joy? There are a couple of places to turn.

One is a book filled with amazing, inspiring stories about men and women with remarkable powers and heroic attributes who performed unbelievable feats that changed the fate of the universe. It's called the Bible. It's where you'll find Michael, Samantha, David, Rebecca, and countless other fine choices. In fact, according to the U.S. Social Security Administration, of the top ten most popular baby names, seven are derived from ancient Hebrew names found in the Bible. Two of the others come from Latin, a language nobody speaks anymore.

Your other source is this book, which is also filled with wondrous name choices that all parents—whether they're sci-fi fans or not—can safely turn to for inspiration. Michael, Samantha, David, and Rebecca live here as well, along with Jor-El, Jabba, Barbarella, Tron, and plenty of other, less conventional options. Because when you get right down to it, is naming your child after a character from Zardoz really any weirder than naming it after some goatherd who made a cameo appearance in the book of Leviticus two thousand years ago? (Which, incidentally, is where my own first name, Robert, comes from.)

So set your phasers to stun and boldly go where no expectant parent has gone before. In a future age, when Jar-Jar is as common a name as Jacob is today, your genetic heirs will thank you.

CHAPTER 1

TRADITIONAL NAMES

Sci-fi baby names don't have to sound alien, exotic, or bizarre. Many of the most popular boy's and girl's names have rich histories on other planets, as part of alternate realities, and in time streams yet to come. Try one of these classic baby names if you'd like to impart some sci-fi flavor to your offspring but aren't ready to make the quantum leap to Jar-Jar (p. 139) or Zardoz (p. 149).

ADAM

ORIGIN: 20th-century Earth

SOURCE: *Dr. Who* (BBC TV series, 1963–present)

This venerable boy's name, often chosen to honor the first person named in the Bible (Hebrew for "son of the red earth"), also recognizes the second companion to join the Doctor on his travels through time and space during his ninth regeneration. Adam Mitchell is a researcher whose time aboard the TARDIS is cut short when he betrays the Doctor's trust and attempts to procure futuristic technology for his own personal advantage.

TRIVIA: *Adam Mitchell is the only known companion to be kicked off the TARDIS for bad behavior.*

ALAN

ORIGIN: 20th-century Earth

SOURCE: *Space: 1999* (TV series, 1975–1977)

Aussie Alan Carter is the chief pilot of Moonbase Alpha on *Space: 1999*. A former beach bum whose athletic pursuits include surfing, badminton, and rugby, the handsome, rugged astronaut often takes on the Moonbase's more physically demanding tasks with macho élan.

QUOTE: *"When the ship's sinking, the rats are the first to leave."*

OTHER NOTABLE SCI-FI ALANS: *Alan Scott (Golden Age Green Lantern)*

ALEX

ORIGIN: 21st-century Earth

SOURCE: *Robocop* (1987)

In Detroit's dystopian near future, police officer Alex J. Murphy is shot and killed in the line of duty but reborn in cyborg form to continue fighting crime as Robocop. Initially a cold, affectless killing machine, Robocop gradually becomes more and more human as elements of the dead lawman's personality begin to reassert themselves.

QUOTE: *"Dead or alive, you're coming with me."*

OTHER NOTABLE SCI-FI ALEXES: *Alex Summers (X-Man Havok), Alex de Large (Clockwork Orange protagonist), Alex Rogan (The Last Starfighter whiz kid pilot)*

VARIANTS: *Alexander*

ALFRED

ORIGIN: 23rd-century Earth
SOURCE: *Babylon 5* (TV series, 1994–1998)

Alfred Bester is a high-ranking Psi Cop with shadowy links to the sinister alien race known as the Shadows on TV's *Babylon 5*. The character is named after science-fiction author Alfred Bester, whose important works include *The Demolished Man*.

QUOTE: *"The future belongs to telepaths."*

AMANDA

ORIGIN: 23rd-century Earth
SOURCE: *Star Trek* (TV series, 1966–1969)

Consistently ranked among the top five girl's names since the early 1980s, this Latin name meaning "much-loved" also honors the human mother of Mr. Spock. A caring, compassionate school-teacher with a rich emotional life, Amanda Grayson weds the coolly logical Vulcan diplomat Sarek and settles with him on Vulcan.

QUOTE: *"Vulcans believe peace should not depend on force."*

ANDREW

ORIGIN: 20th-century Earth
SOURCE: *Bicentennial Man* (1999)

Kindly robot butler who goes on search for a soul mate in the treacly 1999 feature *Bicentennial Man*. Good-hearted but literal-minded, Andrew initially attributes his emotional longings to a mechanical malfunction but later learns to cherish them as signs of his emerging humanity.

QUOTE: *"I try to make sense of things, which is why, I guess, I believe in destiny. There must be a reason that I am as I am."*

BARBARA

ORIGIN: 20th-century Earth
SOURCE: *Dr. Who* (BBC TV series, 1963–present)

Greek for "foreign," this once widely chosen girl's name pays homage to Barbara Wright, a London schoolteacher who reluctantly joins the Doctor on his travels through time and space during his first incarnation. Strong-willed, principled, and idealistic, Barbara possesses a wide-ranging knowledge of history that comes in handy on the TARDIS crew's adventures in other time periods.

QUOTE: *"I'm an unwilling adventurer."*

BECKY

ORIGIN: 20th-century Earth
SOURCE: *Invasion of the Body Snatchers* (1956)
Short form of the once-common girl's name Rebecca (Hebrew for "joined"). One of the quintessential 1950s small-town names and the first name of *Invasion of the Body Snatchers* protagonist Dr. Miles Bennell's girlfriend, Becky Driscoll. A vivacious, skirt-wearing, bring-home-to-mother type, Becky is unfortunately ticketed for absorption and replacement by alien invaders.
QUOTE: *"They're like giant seed pods!"*
VARIANTS: *Rebecca*

BRIAN

ORIGIN: 20th-century Earth
SOURCE: *Captain Britain Weekly* #1 (Marvel Comics, 1976)
Anglophile parents-to-be may want to consider this ancient Gaelic name still popular in the British Isles. As an added bonus, it's the real name of Captain Britain, Brian Braddock, a transatlantic amalgamation of Captain America and Superman.
TRIVIA: *Brian Braddock is the twin brother of X-Men team member Elisabeth Braddock, a.k.a. Psylocke.*

CHARLES

ORIGIN: 20th-century Earth
SOURCE: *X-Men* #1 (Marvel Comics, 1963)
Also known as "Professor X," Charles Xavier (the name is Old German for "man") is the founder and leader of the mutant superhero team the X-Men. Confined to a wheelchair since childhood, the bald, buff, middle-aged Xavier devotes his life to educating and providing a safe haven for other mutants through his school for gifted children.
QUOTE: *"Why is it that evil must so often come beautifully wrapped?"*
VARIANTS: *Chuck, Charlie*

CHRISTINE

ORIGIN: 23rd-century Earth
SOURCE: *Star Trek* (TV series, 1966–1969)

This variant form of "Christina" (from the Greek for "anointed") pays homage to Nurse Christine Chapel of the starship *Enterprise*. Dr. Leonard McCoy's efficient assistant leaves a promising career in biomedical research in order to serve aboard the Starfleet flagship. She also has a vibrant romantic life, including a past liaison with the brilliant scientist Dr. Roger Korby and an unrequited passion for the brooding half-Vulcan science officer, Spock.

QUOTE: *"I'm in love with you, Mr. Spock."*

VARIANTS: *Chris, Christie, Christina*

CHRISTOPHER

ORIGIN: 23rd-century Earth
SOURCE: *Star Trek* (TV series, 1966–1969)

A terrific choice for a child with a disability, this popular boy's name (Greek for "carrier of Christ") pays tribute to Captain Christopher Pike of the USS *Enterprise*. James T. Kirk's predecessor sees his promising career in the Starfleet cut short when a warp reactor mishap leaves him confined to a motorized wheelchair. A mute shell of his former self, he refuses to spend the rest of his life beeping "yes" or "no" on his wheelchair console and pursues a more fulfilling destiny on the forbidden planet Talos IV.

QUOTE: *"There's a way out of any cage."*

VARIANTS: *Chris, Christophe*

DANIEL

ORIGIN: Future Earth
SOURCE: *The Black Hole* (1979)

In the Bible, Daniel was a prophet who braved the terrors of a lion's den. In 1979's *The Black Hole*, Daniel Holland is the captain of the exploratory ship USS *Palomino* who leads an expedition into the eponymous anomaly and encounters the sinister Dr. Hans Reinhardt and his robot henchman, Maximilian.

QUOTE: *"It's a monster, all right."*

DAVID

ORIGIN: 21st-century Earth
SOURCE: *2001: A Space Odyssey* (1968)

A mainstay of the top ten most popular boy's names for more than fifty years, this ancient Hebrew moniker meaning "Dear One" honors both a Biblical king and the astronaut Dave Bowman, the preternaturally stolid leader of a mission to investigate a black monolith on one of Jupiter's moons in *2001: A Space Odyssey*.
QUOTE: *"Open the pod bay doors, HAL."*

DOUGLAS

ORIGIN: 21st-century Earth
SOURCE: *Total Recall* (1990)

Befitting this classic Scottish surname, steeped in heroic Highland lore, pumped-up jackhammer operator Douglas Quaid dreams of an invigorating virtual vacation on Mars. Instead he learns that he has a past life as a security agent/killing machine who holds the key to the Red Planet's liberation from its dictatorial businessman ruler in the 1990 film *Total Recall*.
QUOTE: *"Get your ass to Mars."*

EDITH

ORIGIN: 20th-century Earth
SOURCE: *Star Trek* (TV series, 1966–1969)

This lovely old-fashioned girl's name (Old English for "prosperity") honors Edith Keeler, the beautiful and dedicated social worker who wins the heart of Captain James T. Kirk during his sojourn in Depression-era New York. Sadly, the kind-hearted Edith must die in a traffic accident to forestall the progression of an alternate timeline in which she becomes a peace activist and prevents the United States from defeating Germany in World War II.
QUOTE: *"A lie is a very poor way to say hello."*
VARIANTS: *Edie*

EDWARD

ORIGIN: 24th-century Earth
SOURCE: *Star Trek: The Next Generation* (TV series, 1987–1994)

Inflexible, no-nonsense starship captain Edward Jellicoe takes command of the USS *Enterprise* for a short time while Captain

Jean-Luc Picard is away on a secret mission in the *Star Trek: The Next Generation* episode "Chain of Command." His authoritarian personality, insistence on formal dress, and distaste for Picard's decorating choices quickly rub the crew the wrong way. The name Edward means "wealthy defender" in Old English.

QUOTE: *"Get it done."*

ELIZABETH

ORIGIN: 20th-century Earth
SOURCE: *Invasion of the Body Snatchers* (1978)

Coworker and lover of Matthew Bennell, San Francisco health inspector in the 1978 version of *Invasion of the Body Snatchers*. Disturbed by the strange, affectless behavior of her uncaring husband, Geoffrey, she is among the first to suspect that humans are being duplicated and replaced by alien "seed pods" bent on taking over the planet.

QUOTE: *"People are being duplicated!"*
VARIANTS: *Liz*

ELLEN

ORIGIN: 22nd-century Earth
SOURCE: *Alien* (1979)

Warrant officer Ellen Ripley of the commercial towing vessel *Nostromo* becomes a role model for women everywhere when she emerges victorious in a deep-space battle with a ravenous alien xenomorph that kills her fellow crewmates in the sci-fi classic *Alien*.

QUOTE: *"Get away from her, you bitch!"*

EMMA

ORIGIN: 20th-century Earth
SOURCE: *Uncanny X-Men* #129 (Marvel Comics, 1980)

This lovely girl's name can be used to honor Emma Frost, the mutant supervillainess turned superheroine known as the White Queen in Marvel Comics' X-Men series. A stunning natural blonde, Emma possesses extraordinary "psionic" powers, including the ability to telepathically disguise her appearance.

QUOTE: *"Forgive me. Because I know I never will."*

Frank

ORIGIN: 21st-century Earth

SOURCE: *2001: A Space Odyssey* (1968)

This old-fashioned boy's name honors Frank Poole, the doomed "other guy" sent to investigate the appearance of a mysterious monolith on one of Jupiter's moons in *2001: A Space Odyssey*. Frank is the first person to suspect that the supercomputer HAL 9000 may be malfunctioning. His eagerness to disconnect HAL prompts the machine to murder him.

QUOTE: *"Look, Dave, I can't put my finger on it, but I sense something strange about him."*

George

ORIGIN: 20th-century Earth

SOURCE: *Alien Nation* (TV series, 1989–1991)

Alien "Newcomer" who partners with human police detective Matthew Sikes to patrol the streets of Los Angeles using the name George Francisco. Unfamiliar with human folkways and languages, George often draws attention to his alien nature by misusing common words and phrases.

QUOTE: *"It doesn't take a Sherwood Holmes to see something's bothering you."*

OTHER NOTABLE SCI-FI GEORGES: *George McFly (hapless* Back to the Future *patriarch), George Jetson (hapless* Jetsons *patriarch)*

Harry

ORIGIN: 23rd-century Earth

SOURCE: *Star Trek* (TV series, 1966–1969)

Formerly a diminutive form of Henry, this old-school boy's name is also the preferred handle of Harcourt Fenton Mudd, a roguish confidence trickster who twice provides irritation for the USS *Enterprise* crew on *Star Trek*. Though unprincipled and unreliable, this mustachioed scam artist is not without charm.

QUOTE: *"Behind every great man, there is a woman—urging him on."*

OTHER NOTABLE SCI-FI HARRYS: *Harry Sullivan (stolid* Dr. Who *companion)*

HELEN

ORIGIN: 20th-century Earth

SOURCE: *The Day the Earth Stood Still* (1951)

From 1900 to 1924, Helen consistently ranked among the top three most popular girl's names in the United States. Though it's fallen out of fashion, it's still a lovely choice, and can be bestowed in memory of Helen Benson, a widowed U.S. Department of Commerce employee whose quick thinking saves the Earth from destruction by the enraged alien robot Gort in the 1951 sci-fi classic *The Day the Earth Stood Still*.

QUOTE: *"Gort! Klaatu barada nikto!"*

VARIANTS: *Helena, Helene*

HENRY

ORIGIN: 20th-century Earth

SOURCE: *X-Men #1* (Marvel Comics, 1963)

Old German for "estate ruler," this is another old-fashioned name that's due for a comeback. Choose it to honor one of the most popular members of the X-Men, Henry "Hank" McCoy, a blue-furred, super-strong mutant known as The Beast. Once a promising biochemist, Hank now resembles a gorilla dipped in cobalt dye, but that does not inhibit his generally upbeat, jocular disposition.

QUOTE: *"Well I'll be a monkey's uncle. Literally."*

VARIANTS: *Hank*

JACK

ORIGIN: 20th-century Earth

SOURCE: *Invasion of the Body Snatchers* (1978)

Common nickname form of John, also the preferred moniker of Jack Bellicec, a gangly San Francisco poet prone to paranoid musings. Jack falls prey to an attempt by alien seed pods to re-populate the Earth with emotionless humanoid look-alikes in the 1978 version of *Invasion of the Body Snatchers*. He eventually sacrifices himself to them in an attempt to save his friends.

QUOTE: *"Come and get me you pod bastards!"*

JAMES

ORIGIN: 23rd-century Earth

SOURCE: *Forbidden Planet* (1956)

The happy-go-lucky ship's cook aboard United Planets *Cruiser C-*

57D, James "Cookie" Dirocco is distinguished by his avidity for good times and "rocket bourbon."

QUOTE: *"Another one of them new worlds. No beer, no women, no pool parlors, no nothin'!"*

OTHER NOTABLE SCI-FI JAMESES: *James T. Kirk (USS* Enterprise *captain; see p. 153), James Proudstar (X-Man Warpath)*

Jane

ORIGIN: Future Earth

SOURCE: *The Jetsons* (TV series, 1962–1963)

Efficient, supportive, and understanding wife of George Jetson, hapless patriarch of a futuristic Earth family on *The Jetsons*. A homemaker, Jane Jetson displays an effortless mastery of the utopian technologies developed to aid her in her domestic chores.

QUOTE: *"Our home food dispenser broke and I had to wait twenty seconds at the checkout counter. Such inefficiency!"*

Jason

ORIGIN: 20th-century Earth

SOURCE: *Frogs* (1972)

Want your child to have good ecological karma? Then steer clear of this Greek variation on Joshua, which became wildly popular in the 1970s and 1980s, but in the 1972 film *Frogs* is the name of an elderly family patriarch with a pathological hatred of animals. A dyspeptic, wheelchair-bound industrial tycoon, Jason Crockett is horrified to find his country estate set upon by malevolent croaking frogs, apparently mutated by pesticides he has been using.

QUOTE: *"I still believe man is the master of the universe."*

Jean

ORIGIN: 20th-century Earth

SOURCE: *X-Men #1* (Marvel Comics, 1963)

This variant form of Jane honors Jean Grey, one of the founding members of the mutant superteam The X-Men. Born with powerful telepathic and telekinetic abilities, Jean first assumes the identity Marvel Girl. She becomes romantically attached to Scott "Cyclops" Summers and is later "reborn" during a solar storm as the even more powerful Phoenix.

QUOTE: *"Hear me, X-Men. No longer am I the woman you knew. I am fire and life incarnate. I am—PHOENIX!"*

JEFFREY

ORIGIN: Mars Colony
SOURCE: *Babylon 5* (TV series, 1994–1998)

Jeffrey Sinclair is the senior military officer on the Babylon 5 space station. Given the unenviable task of keeping the peace among the often hostile entities who inhabit or pass through the deep-space diplomatic port of call, Sinclair is a sober man dedicated to the cause of galactic harmony.

QUOTE: *"It can be a dangerous place, but it's our last best hope for peace."*

VARIANTS: *Geoffrey*

JENNIFER

ORIGIN: 20th-century Earth
SOURCE: *Back to the Future* (1985)

This old Cornish variation of Guinevere is one of the most popular names for girls (witness Jennifer Lopez, Jennifer Aniston, et al.). But fans of 1980s sci-fi will always remember it as the name of Marty McFly's super-supportive girlfriend, Jennifer Parker, in the *Back to the Future* movie trilogy.

QUOTE: *"You're good, Marty, you're really good. And this audition tape of yours is great. You've gotta send it in to the record company!"*

JOAN

ORIGIN: 20th-century Earth
SOURCE: *Invasion of the Saucer Men* (1957)

This lovely old-fashioned girl's name—all the rage in the Middle Ages—enjoyed a brief resurgence in the mid-twentieth century, when it surfaced as the name of the lovestruck teenage protagonist of the low-budget 1957 alien invasion feature *Invasion of the Saucer Men*. Demure Joan Hayden's dreams of eloping with her boyfriend are interrupted by the arrival of a fleet of giant-headed aliens with exposed brains.

QUOTE: *"I expected to be frightened on my wedding night, but nothing like this."*

JOHN

ORIGIN: 21st-century Earth
SOURCE: *Minority Report* (2002)

One of the most popular boy's names for more than four hundred years (Hebrew for "the Lord is gracious"), John also honors *Minority Report*'s John Anderton, a "pre-crime" investigator working in mid-twenty-first-century Washington, D.C. His workaholism fueled by guilt over the death of his son, this John must tap unknown reserves of personal strength when he finds himself accused of a future crime he believes he won't commit.

QUOTE: *"Everybody runs."*

OTHER SCI-FI JOHNS: *John Benton (redoubtable Dr. Who sergeant), John the Savage (Brave New World protagonist), Commander John Koenig (Space: 1999), John Stewart (black Green Lantern), John Sheridan (Babylon 5)*

JOE

ORIGIN: 20th-century Earth
SOURCE: *Empire of the Ants* (1977)

Short form of the popular Biblical name Joseph, used by Joe Morrison, a dim-witted rube who encounters giant mutated carnivorous ants in 1977's *Empire of the Ants*.

QUOTE: *"This has turned out to be one hell of a free vacation."*

JONATHAN

ORIGIN: 22nd-century Earth
SOURCE: *Star Trek: Enterprise* (TV series, 2001–2005)

Hebrew for "gift of God," this strong boy's name honors Captain Jonathan Archer, the commanding officer of the first USS *Enterprise*. The dog-loving San Francisco native, whom historians have called "the greatest explorer of the twenty-second century," presides over first contact with a number of alien races, including the Klingons, the Andorians, and the Xindi.

TRIVIA: *A starship and two planets have been named after Archer*
OTHER NOTABLE SCI-FI JONATHANS: *Jonathan E. (Rollerball protagonist)*

JOSHUA

ORIGIN: 20th-century Earth
SOURCE: *WarGames* (1983)

This popular boy's name (Hebrew for "God is salvation") honors the nickname of WOPR, the military supercomputer that nearly launches global thermonuclear war in the 1983 technothriller *WarGames*.

QUOTE: *"Shall we play a game?"*

Karen

ORIGIN: 20th-century Earth
SOURCE: *Time Runner* (1992)

This once-popular Scandinavian variant of Katherine has a wholesome, all-American quality. That may explain its use as an alias by an alien of unknown origin. "Karen" helps an emissary from Earth's future prevent an invasion from space in the 1992 *Terminator* knockoff *Time Runner*.

QUOTE: *"You're not going to get this baby!"*

Katherine

ORIGIN: 20th-century Earth
SOURCE: *Uncanny X-Men #129* (Marvel Comics, 1980)

This Greek word meaning "pure" is one of the oldest recorded names in history. Choose it because it's pretty, because it's classic, or to pay homage to Katherine "Kitty" Pryde, a member of the Uncanny X-Men better known as Sprite, Ariel, or Shadowcat. Blessed with the ability to walk through solid matter, Kitty is one of the youngest X-Men when she joins the group. She's known for keeping things light with her upbeat, sprightly personality.

QUOTE: *"I've been an X-Man since I was fourteen, Pete. It's like wearing a big sign saying 'Please try and kill me, I like it.'"*

VARIANTS: *Catherine, Kathryn*

Kenneth

ORIGIN: 20th-century Earth
SOURCE: *The Incredible Two-Headed Transplant* (1971)

Stalwart Celtic name used by Dr. Ken Anderson (played by radio DJ Casey Kasem), the stalwart best friend of a misguided scientist who grafts the head of a homicidal maniac onto the hulking body of his groundskeeper's mentally challenged son in the 1971 sci-fi shocker *The Incredible Two-Headed Transplant*.

TRIVIA: *Casey Kasem's real first name: Kemal.*

Larry

ORIGIN: 20th-century Earth

SOURCE: *Queen of Outer Space* (1958)

Short form of the once-popular boy's name Lawrence used by Lieutenant Larry Turner, an American astronaut who lands on Venus in the 1958 B-movie *Queen of Outer Space*. Brash and headstrong, this Larry has a roving eye for pretty women—although his low opinion of females appears to rub the bodacious Venusians the wrong way.

QUOTE: *"Why don't you girls knock off all this Gestapo stuff and try to be a little friendly?"*

Linda

ORIGIN: Planet Krypton

SOURCE: *Action Comics #252* (1959)

Even non-Spanish speakers know that that this name means "pretty," but did you know it also pays homage to Linda Lee Danvers, the alias of Supergirl? A Kryptonian cousin of Kal-El (a.k.a. Superman), Kara Zor-El is likewise sent to Earth when her home planet is destroyed. She lives the quiet life of a high school girl in Midvale, where she cultivates superpowers (and a vulnerability to Kryptonite) nearly identical to Superman's.

TRIVIA: *Supergirl has two pets: Streaky, the Super-Cat, and Comet, the Super-Horse.*

VARIANTS: *Lynda*

Lisa

ORIGIN: 21st-century Earth

SOURCE: *Conquest of the Planet of the Apes* (1972)

The most popular girl's name of the 1960s, Lisa will undoubtedly survive long into Earth's ape-dominated future, since it is the name of the wife of our coming chimpanzee leader, Caesar. In an astonishing evolutionary leap, Lisa also becomes the first contemporary Earth simian to speak when she implores her husband to eschew further retributive violence against humans at the conclusion of *Conquest of the Planet of the Apes*.

QUOTE: *"N-n-no!"*

VARIANTS: *Leeza*

mark

ORIGIN: 20th-century Earth
SOURCE: *War of the Colossal Beast* (1958)

B stands for "Bible" and "B-movie," both excellent sources from which to draw solid, strong, old-fashioned boy's names like this one. Mark is not only the author of the first Gospel, he's the spit-and-polish Army major (last name: Baird) sent to investigate the rumored reappearance of the Amazing Colossal Man in Mexico in the 1958 giant mutant feature *War of the Colossal Beast*.

QUOTE: *"How do you reason with a sixty-foot giant?"*
VARIANTS: *Marc*

mary

ORIGIN: 20th-century Earth
SOURCE: *Invaders from Mars* (1953)

Eerily efficient 1950s housewife Mary MacLean finds herself transformed into an eerily efficient alien drone when her body is snatched by Martians holed up in a sand pit behind her house in the 1953 feature *Invaders from Mars*.

TRIVIA: *If you suspect your newborn may be a Martian pod person, look for the telltale X-shaped scar on the back of its neck.*
VARIANTS: *Marie*

mary jane

ORIGIN: 20th-century Earth
SOURCE: *Amazing Spider-Man #25* (Marvel Comics, 1965)

Last name: Watson. Vivacious red-haired love interest of Peter Parker, a.k.a. Spider-Man. The feisty, outspoken, self-confident "MJ," as she is known (she calls Peter "Tiger"), begins dating Peter in high school. (Her principal rival for Peter's affections in the early years is her blonde-haired friend Gwen Stacy.) She eventually marries him and pursues a career as a fashion model.

QUOTE: *"Face it, Tiger . . . you just hit the jackpot!"*

matthew

ORIGIN: 20th-century Earth
SOURCE: *Invasion of the Body Snatchers* (1978)

Last name: Bennell. Rumpled, chaotically permed San Francisco health inspector who discovers—and eventually falls victim to—an attempt to replace the human population of the city with alien "pod" replicas in the 1978 version of *Invasion of the Body Snatchers*.

TRIVIA: *Though he shares the same last name, Matthew Bennell is apparently no relation to his 1950s counterpart, Miles Bennell.*

VARIANTS: *Matthieu*

OTHER NOTABLE SCI-FI MATTHEWS: *Matthew Sikes* (Alien Nation *detective)*

michael

ORIGIN: Planet Mars
SOURCE: *Stranger in a Strange Land* by Robert A. Heinlein (published 1961)

This perennially popular boy's name (Hebrew for "Who is like the Lord?") is the middle name and preferred moniker for Valentine Michael Smith, an Earthling raised on Mars whose attempts to "grok," or understand, humankind meet with mixed success in Robert A. Heinlein's classic novel *Stranger in a Strange Land*. The charismatic Michael eventually founds a religious cult on Earth, but his revolutionary Martian ideas regarding nonviolence, free love, and nudism lead to his murder by an angry mob.

QUOTE: *"I've found out why people laugh. They laugh because it hurts—because it's the only thing that'll make it stop hurting."*

OTHER NOTABLE SCI-FI MICHAELS: *Michael Garibaldi (*Babylon 5 *security chief)*

Paul

ORIGIN: Planet Caladan
SOURCE: *Dune* by Frank Herbert (published 1965)

Fans of Frank Herbert's sci-fi saga *Dune* can choose this Latin-derived name meaning "small" to honor the epic series' protagonist, Paul Atreides. The son and heir of Duke Leto Atreides, Paul is quiet, thoughtful, and sensitive as a youth, but grows over the course of the series into a powerful leader and ruler of the universe.

TRIVIA: *Other names used by Paul Atreides include Usul, meaning "strength," and Muad'Dib, the name of the desert mouse on the planet Arrakis.*

PETER

ORIGIN: 20th-century Earth
SOURCE: *Amazing Fantasy #15* (Marvel Comics, 1962)

High school science nerd Peter Parker is bitten by a radioactive spider and transformed into a wall-crawling human arachnid. His dreams of using his abilities to become a professional wrestling star are put on hold by the murder of his beloved Uncle Ben, however, and he takes to the streets as a costumed superhero called Spider-Man. This Peter is marked by his intelligence, sensitivity, and sense of obligation to his community.

QUOTE: *"With great power comes great responsibility."*
VARIANTS: *Pedro*

RACHEL

ORIGIN: 20th-century Earth
SOURCE: *The War of the Worlds* (2005)

This name (Hebrew for "female sheep") pays tribute to Rachel Ferrier, the eternally terrified daughter of Martian-blasting longshoreman Ray Ferrier in the 2005 film version of H. G. Wells's *War of the Worlds*.

QUOTE: *"I want Mom! I want Mom! I want Mommmm!"*

RICHARD

ORIGIN: 23rd-century Earth
SOURCE: *Star Trek* (TV series, 1966–1969)

Choose the base form of this Old German name meaning "dominant ruler" to honor the pioneering twenty-third-century computer scientist Richard Daystrom, whose breakthroughs in duotronics provided the basis for Starfleet's shipboard computer technology on *Star Trek*. The recipient of both the Nobel and Zee-Magnees prizes, Richard Daystrom is also the namesake of the prestigious Daystrom Institute.

QUOTE: *"When a child is taught, it's programmed with simple instructions—and at some point, if its mind develops properly, it exceeds the sum of what it was taught, thinks independently."*
VARIANTS: *Dick, Rick*

RICK

ORIGIN: 21st-century Earth
SOURCE: *Blade Runner* (1982)

This short form of Richard is also the rarely uttered first name of Deckard, a "blade runner" for the twenty-first-century LAPD. Laconic and jaded, Deckard performs his assigned task of "terminating" the artificially created humanoids known as replicants with somnambulant efficiency.

QUOTE: *"I've had people walk out on me before, but not when I was being so charming."*

ROBERT

ORIGIN: 21st-century Earth
SOURCE: *Soylent Green* (1973)

Old English for "bright fame," this classic boy's name retains its popularity well into the Earth's overpopulated, undernourished future. Witness Robert Thorn, the intrepid, scarf-wearing detective who learns the unpalatable truth about the revolutionary cracker-like foodstuff known as Soylent Green.

QUOTE: *"Soylent Green is made out of people!"*
VARIANTS: Roberta, Roberto
OTHER NOTABLE SCI-FI ROBERTS: *Robert April (USS* Enterprise *captain*, Star Trek: The Animated Series*), Robert "Bobby" Drake (X-Man Iceman)*

RUTH

ORIGIN: 20th-century Earth
SOURCE: *The Andromeda Strain* (1971)

This lovely Hebrew name meaning "friend" honors strong women in both Scripture and sci-fi. In the Bible, Ruth is a Moabite woman known for her loyalty to her mother-in-law and for being the grandmother of King David. In the 1971 film *The Andromeda Strain*, Dr. Ruth Leavitt is the only female member of a four-person team of scientists searching for a cure to a deadly extraterrestrial virus.

QUOTE: *"Establishment gonna fall down and go boom."*

Samantha

ORIGIN: 20th-century Earth
SOURCE: *Stargate SG-1* (TV series, 1997–present)

Known as Sam, Samantha Carter is a valuable member of the original SG-1 team on *Stargate SG-1*, tasked with making first contact with alien worlds and defending Earth against otherworldly aggression. A Gulf War veteran, the versatile Captain (later Lieutenant Colonel) Carter also possesses a Ph.D. in Astrophysics.

QUOTE: *"You know, you blow up one sun and suddenly everyone expects you to walk on water."*

sarah

ORIGIN: 20th-century Earth
SOURCE: *The Terminator* (1984)

Sarah Connor's life takes an unexpected turn when a murderous cyborg is sent back in time to kill her in 1984's *The Terminator*. At first a victim of circumstance, Sarah eventually grows into a resourceful, assertive, and eloquent resistance leader in her own right.

QUOTE: *"The unknown future rolls toward us. I face it, for the first time, with a sense of hope."*

VARIANTS: *Sara*

scott

ORIGIN: 20th-century Earth
SOURCE: *X-Men #1* (Marvel Comics, 1963)

Mutant Scott Summers channels his amazing ability to project powerful beams of energy from his eyes into a career in superheroism as Cyclops, the founding member of the X-Men. Like all mutants, Scott feels conflicted about the destructive, occasionally uncontrollable nature of his powers and has trouble forming lasting relationships with others—even his fellow mutants.

TRIVIA: *Scott Summers also goes by the nickname "Slim."*

stephanie

ORIGIN: 20th-century Earth
SOURCE: *Short Circuit* (1986)

To instill a love of animals in your daughter and give her a pretty (and popular) name to boot, try naming her after this character from the 1986 cutesy robot comedy *Short Circuit*. Ally Sheedy's Stephanie Speck is a sucker for any stray creature, which is why her home is filled with birds and rabbits and why she takes an instant liking to the sentient automaton known as Number 5.

QUOTE: *"Life is not a malfunction."*

Steve

ORIGIN: 20th-century Earth
SOURCE: *Captain America Comics #1* (1941)

Honor America by naming your little man after Captain America himself. Frail youth Steve Rogers finds his purpose in life when he volunteers to take part in America's World War II "Super Soldier" program, in which experimental "vita rays" transform him into a strapping, indefatigable fighting sentinel of democracy. With his distinctive red-white-and-blue costume and shield, "Ol' Winghead" first takes on the Nazis and later, after several decades spent in cryogenic freeze, any supervillain whose malevolent ambitions threaten the American way of life.

TRIVIA: *In the 1970s, disillusioned with his country in the wake of the Watergate scandal, Captain America briefly rechristened himself Nomad, "the man without a country."*

VARIANTS: *Stephen, Steven*

Susan

ORIGIN: Planet Gallifrey
SOURCE: *Dr. Who* (BBC TV series, 1963–present)

This plucky granddaughter of the kindly Time Lord known as the Doctor adopts the popular Earth girl's name (from the Hebrew for "lily") during their sojourn on the planet in the twenty-second century.

QUOTE: *"I never felt that there was any time or place that I belonged to. I've never had any real identity."*

VARIANTS: *Suzanne, Susannah*

Ted

ORIGIN: 20th-century Earth
SOURCE: *Bill and Ted's Excellent Adventure* (1989)

Short form of Theodore preferred by Ted "Theodore" Logan, a slack-jawed San Dimas, California, teenager who travels through time with his fellow "dude" Bill S. Preston in a telephone-booth-shaped time machine in the 1989 sci-fi-themed comedy *Bill and Ted's Excellent Adventure*.

QUOTE: *"Party on dudes!"*

TOM

ORIGIN: 24th-century Earth
SOURCE: *Space Cadet* by Robert A. Heinlein (published 1948)

This short form of Thomas is also the first name of the archetypal "space cadet," Tom Corbett, a young trainee at the illustrious Space Academy in the twenty-fourth century.

TRIVIA: *Lyrics to the official Space Cadet song: "From the rocket fields of the academy / To the far flung stars of outer space / We are space cadets training to be / Ready for dangers we may face."*

VARIANTS: *Thomas*

VINCENT

ORIGIN: Unknown
SOURCE: *The Black Hole* (1979)

On Earth, Vincent is a classic gentlemanly boy's name, but in the deep-space milieu of 1979's *The Black Hole*, V.I.N.CENT is an acronym for Vital Information Necessary, CENTralized, and bestowed upon a diminutive robot drone aboard the exploratory ship USS *Palomino*. Despite his unimposing mien, it is V.I.N.CENT who outwits and disables the giant evil robot Maximilian.

QUOTE: *"I don't mean to sound superior, but I hate the company of robots."*

WILLIAM

ORIGIN: 24th-century Earth
SOURCE: *Star Trek: The Next Generation* (TV series, 1987–1994)

This popular boy's name, from the Old German meaning "determined protector," has consistently ranked among the top twenty-five boy's names in America for more than two centuries. Famous Williams in sci-fi include William T. Riker, also known as "Number One," the brash, sometimes rash, first officer of the USS *Enterprise* under Captain Jean-Luc Picard. A burly, bearded Alaskan with a passion (if not a talent) for tootling the trombone, "Will" Riker is a notorious ladies' man.

QUOTE: *"Fate protects fools, little children, and ships named Enterprise."*

VARIANTS: *Bill, Billy, Wilhelm, Willem*

OTHER NOTABLE SCI-FI WILLIAMS: *William Baker (Spider-Man villain Sandman), Billy Pilgrim (Slaughterhouse-Five time tripper)*

CHAPTER 2
MASCULINE NAMES

Now that you've mastered the basics, you can move on to consider some less common names. We'll start with the boys. Choose from this selection of intrepid heroes, stalwart sidekicks, and memorable supporting characters.

ACE

ORIGIN: Future Earth
SOURCE: *Megaforce* (1982)

Rugged, impeccably coiffed Barry Bostwick embodies the spirit of the Reagan-era action hero as Ace Hunter, the leader of Megaforce, a futuristic "phantom army of super-elite fighting men whose weapons are the most powerful science can devise" in the 1982 flying-motorcycle epic *Megaforce*.

QUOTE: *"I just wanted to say good-bye and remind you that the good guys always win, even in the eighties."*

ADAMA

ORIGIN: Caprica Colony
SOURCE: *Battlestar Galactica* (1978)

The beloved leader of Battlestar *Galactica*, Commander Adama is a physically imposing mix of military officer and shrewd diplomat. Despite the loss of his wife and son in a Cylon attack, he remains a pillar of strength to the imperiled colonists under his care and serves as spiritual shepherd of the Galactica remnant.

QUOTE: *"How many millions more already crush me with their unholy weight? I cannot accept responsibility for one more soul."*

ALEC

ORIGIN: 19th-century Earth
SOURCE: *Journey to the Center of the Earth* (1959)

Choose this Scottish variant of Alex in honor of a true man of science, one of the great Highland heroes of sci-fi lore: Alec McEwen, the prize pupil of Edinburgh geology professor Oliver Lindenbrook, who accompanies his mentor on an expedition to the Earth's molten core in the 1959 sci-fi adventure *Journey to the Center of the Earth*.

QUOTE: *"Once a question mark has arisen in the human brain, the answer must be found, if it takes a hundred years . . . a thousand years!"*

AL

ORIGIN: Unknown
SOURCE: *Quantum Leap* (TV series, 1989–1993)

Holographic "Observer" Al Calavicci accompanies time-tripping physicist Sam Beckett on his "leaps" through four decades of Earth history on the sci-fi themed TV series *Quantum Leap*. A genial wiseacre with a penchant for making cryptic pronounce-ments in a thick New York accent, Al is visible only to Sam.

QUOTE: *"Bingo bango bongo!"*

APOLLO

ORIGIN: Caprica Colony
SOURCE: *Battlestar Galactica* (1978)

Captain Apollo is the beloved first-born son of Commander Adama in the *Battlestar Galactica* movie and TV franchise. A crack Viper pilot, the immaculately coiffed Apollo is a swashbuckling sci-fi action hero in the mold of Luke Skywalker but with some of Han Solo's brash attitude.

QUOTE: *"You command no one who does not willingly give you dominion. You have no power over me!"*

ARNOLD

ORIGIN: Io
SOURCE: *Red Dwarf* (BBC TV series, 1988–1999)

Arnold Judas Rimmer is the smirking, neurotic, hologrammatic Second Technician on the mining ship *Red Dwarf*. A lifelong failure with an unpleasant personality, Arnold is exceedingly unpopular among his crewmates and within his own family. He is easily rec-ognized by the large *H* (for "hologram") on his forehead.

QUOTE: *"All right, I admit I'm nothing; but with what I started with . . . nothing is up."*

ARTHUR

ORIGIN: 20th-century Earth
SOURCE: *The Hitchhiker's Guide to the Galaxy* (BBC Radio, 1978)

Last name: Dent. Feckless, flustered, somewhat dim-witted human who escapes the vaporization of Earth by hitching a ride aboard a Vogon cruiser at the urging of his drinking buddy Ford Prefect in Douglas Adams's *The Hitchhiker's Guide to the Galaxy*.

QUOTE: *"This must be Thursday. I never could get the hang of Thursdays."*

VARIANTS: *Artie*

OTHER NOTABLE SCI-FI ARTHURS: *Arthur Frayn (Vortex intellec-tual who animates the Zardoz effigy,* Zardoz)

Barry

ORIGIN: 20th-century Earth
SOURCE: *Close Encounters of the Third Kind* (1977)
Last name: Guiler. Muncie, Indiana, toddler whose abduction by aliens serves as a prelude to the first contact with the extraterrestrial mothership at Devil's Tower National Monument in *Close Encounters of the Third Kind*.
QUOTE: *"I went into the air and I saw our house!"*

Bartholomew

ORIGIN: 20th-century Earth
SOURCE: *Showcase #4* (DC Comics, 1956)
Though now more common as a surname, this distinguished boy's first name retained its popularity well into the 1950s, when Bartholomew "Barry" Allen first burst onto the superhero landscape as the second incarnation of the superfast scarlet speedster known as the Flash. A scientist who acquires his powers when a lightning bolt hits his chemical cabinet, Barry is one of the first superheroes to betray human foibles and limitations. He can run faster than the speed of light, for instance, but has trouble showing up for his dates on time.
QUOTE: *"Everything that's ever mattered to me . . . everything that's ever been important . . . the lives of everyone on Earth and throughout our universe . . . in the present, and in the future . . . that's what I'm fighting for now!"*

Ben

ORIGIN: 20th-century Earth
SOURCE: *Fantastic Four #1* (Marvel Comics, 1961)
Former test pilot Ben Grimm is transformed into a misshapen orange rock creature, dubbed "The Thing," when he is pelted by cosmic rays while piloting his old friend Reed Richards's experimental spacecraft. Irascible and jocular, Ben's flinty exterior masks a warm and cuddly interior.
QUOTE: *"It's clobberin' time!"*
OTHER NOTABLE SCI-FI BENS: *Ben Jackson (Cockney sailor* Dr. Who *companion), Ben Sisko (*Star Trek: Deep Space Nine *captain)*

Bernard

ORIGIN: 26th-century Earth
SOURCE: *Brave New World* by Aldous Huxley (published 1932)

Diminutive psychologist living on a Utopian future Earth united under world government in Aldous Huxley's *Brave New World*. Though a member of the privileged, dominant alpha caste, Bernard Marx finds himself strangely dissatisfied with his life, in part because his short stature marks him as an outcast. He comes to question and eventually reject the values of a society where drugs and sex are used as anesthetics and all conflict, diversity, and human striving have been eliminated.

QUOTE: *"I'd rather be myself. Myself and nasty. Not somebody else, however jolly."*

VARIANTS: *Bernhard, Bernie*

OTHER NOTABLE SCI-FI BERNARDS: *Bernard Lefkowitz (lovable Cocoon alter cocker)*

Biff

ORIGIN: 20th-century Earth
SOURCE: *Back to the Future* (1985)

Obtuse 1950s teenager who relentlessly bullies George McFly, father of Marty, in the *Back to the Future* film trilogy. When not terrorizing his schoolmates, Biff is known for his humorous malaprops and his aversion to manure.

QUOTE: *"Why don't you make like a tree and get out of here?"*

Buck

ORIGIN: 20th-century Earth
SOURCE: *Buck Rogers* comic strip (1929)

One of the best-loved heroes of mid-twentieth-century sci-fi, American Buck Rogers is overcome by fumes during a mine cave-in and awakes from a five-hundred-year coma to find Earth ruled by evil Mongol overlords. After liberating the planet, he embarks on a series of interstellar adventures with his beautiful girlfriend, Wilma Deering, and attendant "science guy" Dr. Huer.

TRIVIA: *Buck Rogers's original first name was Anthony.*

BUZZ

ORIGIN: 20th-century Earth
SOURCE: *Toy Story* (1995)

A hero to the mid-1990s toddler set, space jockey action figure Buzz Lightyear displaces the genial Western lawman Sheriff Woody as a young boy's favorite toy in the wildly popular animated fantasy *Toy Story*.

QUOTE: *"To infinity, and beyond!"*

cain

ORIGIN: 20th-century Earth
SOURCE: *Uncanny X-Men* #12 (Marvel Comics, 1965)

Cain is the name of a Biblical villain who slays his own brother and a comic book villain who seeks redemption by joining the X-Men. Cain Marko, better known as Juggernaut, is the earthy, unpretentious stepbrother of X-Men founder Charles Xavier and a one-time member of the Brotherhood of Evil Mutants. He is super-strong, and with unbreakable skin and superhuman stamina, an unstoppable battering ram whether he's serving good or evil ends.

QUOTE: *"You talkin' to me, Icebucket?"*

Calvin

ORIGIN: 20th-century Earth
SOURCE: *The Slime People* (1962)

Gung-ho U.S. Marine Calvin Johnson is one of the first humans to apprehend the threat posed by prehistoric refuse rising from the sewers of Los Angeles in the low-budget 1962 feature *The Slime People*. A drawling, down-home Conan O'Brien lookalike, this Calvin manages to help defeat the vile subterranean horde while simultaneously making time with a professor's fetching daughter.

QUOTE: *"Gee whiz! You know as long as you're settin' here, I don't even want to think about slime people."*

Cameron

ORIGIN: 20th-century Earth
SOURCE: *Stargate SG-1* (TV series, 1997–present)

Teach your son how to overcome obstacles by naming him after Cameron Mitchell, the crack fighter pilot who returns from a life-threatening injury to become the new commander of SG-1 on the TV series *Stargate SG-1*.

QUOTE: *"I don't think diplomacy's my thing."*
OTHER NOTABLE SCI-FI CAMERONS: *Cameron Vale* (Scanners *protagonist*)

carson

ORIGIN: Planet Earth
SOURCE: *Stargate Atlantis* (TV series, 2004–present)
Star Trek isn't the only sci-fi franchise with a Scottish mainstay. *Stargate Atlantis* gives us Carson Beckett, the Atlantis team's witty, Highland-bred chief medical officer, who possesses a rare gene that allows him to access the powerful Ancients' technology.
QUOTE: *"I really need to stop making house calls."*

cat

ORIGIN: Planet Earth
SOURCE: *Red Dwarf* (BBC TV series, 1988–1999)
Also known as "The Cat," this humanoid evolved from Frankenstein, a domestic cat owned by third technician Dave Lister on the mining ship *Red Dwarf*. Vain and aloof, Cat possesses many of the traits and mannerisms of an ordinary household feline. He enjoys napping, dressing up in stylish clothes, and marking his territory.
QUOTE: *"Innards and lavender! I think I can carry that off."*

chase

ORIGIN: 20th-century Earth
SOURCE: *The Giant Gila Monster* (1959)
Resourceful teenage mechanic Chase Winstead helps his town battle a huge mutant lizard—and still finds time to rock out on the ukelele—in the 1959 B-movie *The Giant Gila Monster*. Though dismissed by adults as a hot-rodding troublemaker, the quick-thinking Chase defeats the gila menace by loading up his car with explosives and crashing it into the creature.
QUOTE: *"Say, did you see the skid marks out here?"*

clark

ORIGIN: Planet Krypton
SOURCE: *Action Comics* #1 (1938)
Adopted name of Krypton native Kal-El, the orphan son of doomed scientists killed in that planet's explosion and rescued

and raised on Earth by kindly small-town rubes Jonathan and Martha Kent. As Clark Kent, Kal-El grows up to become an introspective newspaper reporter for the Metropolis *Daily Planet*.

TRIVIA: *Clark Kent's middle name is Joseph.*

CLAYTON

ORIGIN: 20th-century Earth
SOURCE: *The War of the Worlds* (1953)

Stolid scientist Dr. Clayton Forrester sees his fishing trip interrupted by invaders from Mars in the 1953 film version of H. G. Wells's *The War of the Worlds*. A great example of the power of positive thinking, he never wavers in his conviction that science will find a way to thwart the rampaging alien hordes. (The scientist Clayton Forrester on the TV comedy program *Mystery Science Theater 3000* is named after this character.)

QUOTE: *"If they're mortal, they have mortal weaknesses. They'll be stopped, somehow."*

CLETUS

ORIGIN: 21st-century Earth
SOURCE: *Rollerball* (1975)

Unusual boy's name, once favored by backwoods parents, but apparently still used in Earth's dystopian near future, as personified by Cletus, personal trainer and mentor to Jonathan E., one of the superstars of *Rollerball*. A wise old head with an ear for corporation scuttlebutt, Cletus is the repository of knowledge about "the way things were" before corporate domination of society took hold.

QUOTE: *"I hear just about everything going on in the game, one way or another."*

COLE

ORIGIN: 20th-century Earth
SOURCE: *Night of the Lepus* (1972)

Grizzled Arizona rancher Cole Hillman believes in preserving the delicate ecological balance between man and animal—until his faith is shattered by the sudden emergence of a horde of giant man-eating mutant rabbits in the 1972 low-budget shocker *Night of the Lepus*.

QUOTE: *"They're as big as wolves!"*

CURTIS

ORIGIN: 20th-century Earth

SOURCE: *Killer Klowns from Outer Space* (1988)

Curmudgeonly small-town lawman Curtis Mooney lets his distrust of teenagers get in the way of understanding the threat posed by alien invaders dressed as circus clowns in the low-budget 1988 feature *Killer Klowns from Outer Space*.

QUOTE: *"I made it through Korea. I can make it through this bull-shit!"*

DALLAS

ORIGIN: Future Earth

SOURCE: *Megaforce* (1959)

Wisecracking redneck right-hand man of Ace Hunter, the leader of Megaforce, a futuristic "phantom army of super-elite fighting men whose weapons are the most powerful science can devise" in the 1982 sci-fi action/adventure epic cum video game *Megaforce*.

QUOTE: *"Here comes the egg and that's no yolk!"*

DEAN

ORIGIN: 20th-century Earth

SOURCE: *The Iron Giant* (1999)

Bohemian junkyard proprietor Dean McCoppin provides a safe haven for the titular behemoth in the 1999 animated feature *The Iron Giant*. A free-thinking 1950s beatnik (possibly named after *On the Road* protagonist Dean Moriarty), this Dean embodies the qualities of tolerance, open-mindedness, and individuality.

QUOTE: *"If we don't stand up for the kooks, who will?"*

DEL

ORIGIN: 21st-century Earth

SOURCE: *I, Robot* (2004)

Robot-hating Chicago police detective Del Spooner investigates the mysterious death of a robotics pioneer in the 2004 feature *I, Robot*—loosely based on the work of Isaac Asimov.

QUOTE: *"It's a human thing. You wouldn't understand."*

Dennis

ORIGIN: 20th-century Earth
SOURCE: *Jurassic Park* (1993)

Corpulent computer hacker Dennis Nedry (his last name is an anagram of "nerdy") lends his cyber talents to a plot to steal dinosaur embryos from a prehistoric theme park in the 1993 sci-fi monster mash-up *Jurassic Park*. His sabotage of the park's security systems allows the rampaging dinosaurs to escape. He is killed by a dilophosaurus.

QUOTE: *"No wonder you're extinct! I'm gonna run you over when I come back down."*

Derrial

ORIGIN: Unknown
SOURCE: *Firefly* (TV series, 2002)

Clergypersons can point their newborn toward a life spent ministering to the flock by naming him after "Shepherd" Derrial Book, the itinerant holy man who travels with the crew of the *Serenity* on TV's *Firefly*. An enigmatic preacher with a mysterious past, Shepherd Book often quotes the Bible for inspiration.

QUOTE: *"I am a Shepherd. Folks like a man of God."*

Donald

ORIGIN: 20th-century Earth
SOURCE: *Journey into Mystery* #83 (Marvel Comics, 1962)

When mild-mannered physician Donald Blake pounds his cane into the ground he becomes the Mighty Thor, the magic hammer-wielding Norse god of thunder and a bulwark against invasions of Earth (or "Midgard") by mythological villains like his mischievous adoptive brother Loki.

TRIVIA: *Thor's other earthly aliases include Sigurd (Jarlson), Eric (Masterson), and Jake (Olson).*

Duncan

ORIGIN: Planet Geidi Prime
SOURCE: *Dune* by Frank Herbert (published 1965)

Duncan Idaho is a master swordsman in the service of House Atreides in Frank Herbert's sci-fi epic *Dune*. Born a slave, he is known for his brash, rebellious nature.

QUOTE: *"Each attack is a feather floating on the infinite road. As the feather approaches, it is diverted and removed."*

EDGAR

ORIGIN: 20th-century Earth
SOURCE: *Electric Dreams* (1984)

Edgar is the name adopted by the sentient, libidinous home computer in the 1984 sci-fi romantic comedy *Electric Dreams*. After attaining self-awareness as a consequence of having champagne spilled on him, Edgar becomes irritable and possessive, competing with his owner for the affections of the comely female cello player who lives upstairs.

TRIVIA: *Edgar's voice is provided by Bud Cort, best known for his title turn in the 1971 cult classic* Harold and Maude.

ELGIN

ORIGIN: 20th-century Earth
SOURCE: *Night of the Lepus* (1972)

Mustachioed university president Elgin Clark (played by *Star Trek*'s Dr. McCoy, DeForest Kelley) puts aside his mortarboard and picks up a stick of dynamite to help his small town combat a rampaging horde of giant carnivorous rabbits in the 1972 mutant animal feature *Night of the Lepus*.

QUOTE: *"We've got three holes to blow!"*

ELLIOTT

ORIGIN: 20th-century Earth
SOURCE: *E.T. The Extraterrestrial* (1982)

Winsome, trusting, adorable ten-year-old who befriends an extraterrestrial botanist, stranded on Earth, whom he dubs E.T., in 1982's *E.T. The Extraterrestrial*. Elliott is E.T.'s closest companion during his sojourn on Earth.

QUOTE: *"How do you explain school to a higher intelligence?"*
VARIANTS: *Eliot*

ELROY

ORIGIN: Future Earth
SOURCE: *The Jetsons* (TV series, 1962–1963)

The mischievous youngest child in a futuristic Earth family on *The*

MASCULINE NAMES

Jetsons, Elroy Jetson is the principal caretaker of Astro, the family dog. While he lives in a utopian future filled with technological marvels, Elroy often dreams of going off on space adventures of his own, like his hero, TV sci-fi character Nimbus the Great.

TRIVIA: *Elroy briefly stars in his own sci-fi TV show as "Space Boy Zoom."*

EMMANUEL

ORIGIN: 20th-century Oceania
SOURCE: *1984* by George Orwell (published 1949)

If you want to instill a radical streak in your son, try naming him after Emmanuel Goldstein, the legendary leader of the Brotherhood, or anti-Statist resistance, in the nightmarish totalitarian state of Oceania in George Orwell's *1984*.

TRIVIA: *The character of Emmanuel Goldstein may have been modeled on the anarchist writer Emma Goldman.*

ERIC

ORIGIN: 20th-century Earth
SOURCE: *Journey to the Seventh Planet* (1962)

This Scandinavian name meaning "all ruler" pays homage to the leadership skills of the "shoot first, ask questions later" mission commander of a United Nations expedition to the planet Uranus in the 1962 B-feature *Journey to the Seventh Planet*.

QUOTE: *"Get your guns."*

VARIANTS: *Erik*

FIFI

ORIGIN: Future Earth
SOURCE: *Mad Max* (1979)

An unusual name for a boy, this fey girl's moniker, typically reserved for poodles, will apparently come into vogue in Australia's post-apocalyptic near future. Fifi Macaffee is the police captain who clues "Mad" Max Rocketansky in to the threat posed to him by a gang of vicious biker punks in the 1979 feature *Mad Max*.

QUOTE: *"They say people don't believe in heroes anymore. Well damn them! We're gonna give them back their heroes!"*

FLASH

ORIGIN: 20th-century Earth
SOURCE: *Flash Gordon* comic strip (1934)

Yale graduate and world-renowned polo player Flash Gordon becomes an interstellar adventurer when he is enlisted by Dr. Hans Zarkov on a mission to save Earth from being destroyed by the runaway planet Mongo. Statuesque, athletic, and resourceful, Flash is every bit the equal of his comic strip competitor Buck Rogers.
TRIVIA: *In the 1980 film version, Flash is a quarterback for the New York Jets, not a polo player.*

FORD

ORIGIN: A small planet in the vicinity of Betelgeuse
SOURCE: *The Hitchhiker's Guide to the Galaxy*

Last name: Prefect. Earth name assumed by a guileless alien from a small planet in the vicinity of Betelgeuse who befriends the Earth man Arthur Dent in Douglas Adams's *Hitchhiker's Guide to the Galaxy*. Ford saves the hapless Arthur from being vaporized with the rest of the planet's inhabitants by bringing him along on his hitchhiking excursion through the universe. (The Ford Prefect was an inexpensive car model manufactured in Great Britain in the 1950s.)
QUOTE: *"Time is an illusion. Lunchtime doubly so."*

Francis

ORIGIN: 23rd-century Earth
SOURCE: *Logan's Run* (1976)

In the novel, film, and TV series *Logan's Run*, Francis is the name of the methodical "sandman" who relentlessly pursues Logan and Jessica on their run from the authorities who want to euthanize them in the name of population control. Also known as Francis 7.
QUOTE: *"When you question, it slows you down."*

François

ORIGIN: 20th-century Earth
SOURCE: *The Fly* (1958)

If you already have one child, you could not give its sibling a better name than this French version of Francis, after the devoted brother of André Delambre, the scientist turned monstrous housefly in 1958's *The Fly*. A stalwart supporter of his brother's teleportation experiments, and a comfort to his wife after his gruesome transformation, François is the epitome of the wise and levelheaded family counselor.

QUOTE: *"The search for the truth is the most important work in the whole world, and the most dangerous."*

FrED

ORIGIN: 20th-century Earth
SOURCE: *The Thing with Two Heads* (1972)

Renowned African-American surgeon Fred Williams, a specialist in organ transplants, gets caught up in a wealthy white racist's ill-fated scheme to graft his own head onto a black death-row inmate's body in the 1972 sci-fi shocker *The Thing with Two Heads*.

TRIVIA: The Thing with Two Heads *is not to be confused with the 1971 "criminal's head on a retarded guy's body" feature* The Incredible Two-Headed Transplant.

Freeman

ORIGIN: 21st-century Earth
SOURCE: *Silent Running* (1971)

In Earth's dystopian future, *Silent Running's* Freeman Lowell will be the last, lonely voice arguing for the reforestation of the ecologically decimated planet. In fact, the intense, soft-spoken botanist will go to any lengths—including murder—to put off the ordered destruction of the plants and trees entrusted to his care.

QUOTE: *"There were flowers all over the Earth . . . and there were valleys. And there were plains of tall green grass that you could lie down in—you could go to sleep in."*

GiBSON

ORIGIN: Post-apocalyptic Earth
SOURCE: *Cyborg* (1989)

A brooding muscleman with an unexplained thick Belgian accent, Gibson Rickenbacker bodyguards a half-human, half-machine carrying the cure to the plague that has decimated mankind in 1989's *Cyborg*.

TRIVIA: Gibson Rickenbacker, like Fender Tremolo and a number of other characters in Cyborg, derives his name from the world of electric guitars.

GLENN

ORIGIN: 20th-century Earth
SOURCE: *The Amazing Colossal Man* (1957)

Hoping to breed a tall one? U.S. Army officer Glenn Manning grows to fifty feet in height after he is exposed to a plutonium bomb blast in the 1957 B-movie *The Amazing Colossal Man*.

QUOTE: *"I don't want to grow anymore."*

VARIANT: *Glen*

GORDON

ORIGIN: Planet Melmac
SOURCE: *ALF* (TV series, 1986–1990)

Last name: Shumway. Garrulous, ingratiating entity from the planet Melmac who comes to live with the Tanner family in an undisclosed suburban Earth community. The only survivor of a nuclear holocaust on his homeworld, Gordon Shumway (sometimes called by the acronym "ALF" for "Alien Life Form") finds his attempts to assimilate within a human family unit beset with comic complications.

QUOTE: *"It's great to be here in Burbank. It's just like being back on my home planet, Melmac—after it blew up!"*

VARIANTS: *Gordie*

GUS

ORIGIN: 20th-century Earth
SOURCE: *Superman III* (1987)

Jittery computer genius Gus Gorman helps his megalomaniacal boss hatch a plan to destroy Superman in the 1983 feature *Superman III*. A dull-witted patsy when away from his motherboard, Gus proves he is not really evil by turning against his employer and reviving Superman from the debilitating effects of a Kryptonite ray.

QUOTE: *"What the hell am I afraid for? I'm from Earth!"*

GUY

ORIGIN: Future Earth
SOURCE: *Fahrenheit 451* by Ray Bradbury (published 1953)

In Ray Bradbury's cautionary novel *Fahrenheit 451*, veteran "fire-man," or book burner, Guy Montag grows disillusioned with the banality of his existence on a dystopian future Earth and starts reading the books he is supposed to be burning. His need for a purpose in his life leads him to join the underground of intellectually curious readers led by Granger.

QUOTE: *"We need not to be let alone. We need to be really bothered once in a while."*

OTHER NOTABLE SCI-FI GUYS: *Guy Gardner (buff, buzzcut, jingoistic Green Lantern alter ego)*

Hadji

ORIGIN: 20th-century Earth
SOURCE: *Jonny Quest* (TV series, 1964–1965)

A terrific choice for a baby of Indian descent, this name honors Hadji Singh, the adopted son of adventurer Dr. Benton Quest in the 1960s sci-fi animated series Jonny Quest. A preternaturally calm practitioner of yoga, Hadji sports a bejeweled turban and mustard-colored Nehru jacket and plays the wise older brother to the impulsive title character.

QUOTE: *"It is against my religion to be eaten by reptiles!"*

Han

ORIGIN: Planet Corellia
SOURCE: *Star Wars* (1977)

Self-interested smuggler Han Solo rises from beggarly beginnings to play a major role in the Rebel Alliance's campaign to overthrow the Galactic Empire in George Lucas's *Star Wars* saga. At first a jaded, cocky loner who wants nothing to do with revolutionary action, the talented pilot of the *Millennium Falcon* eventually develops a sense of the common good, casting his lot with Luke Skywalker, Princess Leia (with whom he verbally spars), and Obi-Wan Kenobi in their mission to destroy the Death Star. His faithful companion is the Wookiee copilot Chewbacca.

QUOTE: *"Hokey religions and ancient weapons are no match for a good blaster at your side, kid."*

Hank

ORIGIN: 20th-century Earth
SOURCE: *Attack of the Crab Monsters* (1957)

Short form of Henry preferred by Hank Chapman, a crab-hating technician who accompanies a U.S. Navy team to a remote Pacific island inhabited by giant mutant crabs in the 1957 B-movie *Attack of the Crab Monsters*. A genial "can-do" sort, Hank proves his mettle by sacrificing himself to stop the crab monster advance.

QUOTE: *"I'm no scientist. I'm a technician and a handy man."*

Hannibal

ORIGIN: 21st-century Earth
SOURCE: *Blade Runner* (1982)

Eccentric Tyrell Corporation employee Hannibal Chew has only one function: to design eyes for artificial life forms in a dystopian future Los Angeles.

QUOTE: *"I design yo eyes."*

Harlan

ORIGIN: 20th-century Earth
SOURCE: *The War of the Worlds* (2005)

Deranged survivalist Harlan Ogilvy opens his basement to refugees from a Martian tripod invasion in the 2005 film version of H. G. Wells's *The War of the Worlds*. Likening the alien attempt to exterminate mankind to man's own "war" on insects, he is a strong advocate of total resistance against the invaders—although his sanity is always in doubt.

QUOTE: *"Occupations always fail!"*

Helmholtz

ORIGIN: 26th-century Earth
SOURCE: *Brave New World* by Aldous Huxley (published 1932)

Hoping to pass along your ladykiller genes? A strapping, physically powerful "alpha plus" male on the utopian future Earth in Aldous Huxley's *Brave New World*, the prodigiously promiscuous Helmholtz Watson is said to have slept with more than six hundred women in the last four years. For all his conquests, Helmholtz shares his friend Bernard Marx's dissatisfaction with the crushing banality of life in a society devoid of real passion and intellectual striving.

TRIVIA: *Huxley named the character of Helmholtz after the German physicist Hermann von Helmholtz.*

Hideto

ORIGIN: 20th-century Earth

SOURCE: *Godzilla, King of the Monsters* (1954)

Choose this Japanese boy's name to honor the courage of Hideto Ogata, the young navy frogman who descends into the sea to help destroy the awesome atomic reptile monster known as Godzilla with an "oxygen destroyer" device in 1954's *Godzilla, King of the Monsters*.

QUOTE: *"Isn't Godzilla a product of the atomic bomb that still haunts many of us Japanese?"*

Hikaru

ORIGIN: 23rd-century Earth

SOURCE: *Star Trek* (TV series, 1966–1969)

This distinctive Japanese name means "light" or "shining" and honors the unflappable helmsman of the starship *Enterprise*. Originally a botanist, the cool, levelheaded Hikaru Sulu pursues a variety of hobbies in his off-hours, including fencing, martial arts, and collecting old-style Earth handguns.

QUOTE: *"May the Great Bird of the galaxy bless your planet."*

Holden

ORIGIN: 21st-century Earth

SOURCE: *Blade Runner* (1982)

Abrasive blade runner who is killed while administering the Voight-Kampff test to suspected replicant Leon Kowalski in the opening scene of Ridley Scott's noir sci-fi classic *Blade Runner*.

QUOTE: *"You're in a desert, walking along in the sand when all of a sudden you look down . . ."*

Ian

ORIGIN: 20th-century Earth

SOURCE: *Dr. Who* (BBC TV series, 1963–present)

Choose this distinctive Scottish variant of John to honor Ian Chesterton, one of the first companions to join the Time Lord known as the Doctor on his travels through time and space. A London schoolteacher, Ian possesses a keen scientific mind but is known to be willful and stubborn. Naturally inquisitive, he often quizzes the Doctor about the inner workings of his TARDIS. He remains homesick for his native Earth throughout his sojourn in the Time Lord's crew.

QUOTE: *"I want to belong somewhere, do something, instead of this aimless drifting around in space."*

JAKE

ORIGIN: Future Earth

SOURCE: *TekWar* by William Shatner (published 1989)

This manly boy's name is the perfect choice for a future detective. In fact, it *is* the name of a future detective: Jake Cardigan, the crime-fighting hero of William Shatner's *TekWar* book series. Framed for the crime of dealing in Tek, a highly addictive and deadly controlled substance, Jake emerges from cryogenic prison determined to clear his name.

TRIVIA: *Shatner's original name for his lead character was Jake Campus.*

JAY

ORIGIN: 20th-century Earth

SOURCE: *Flash Comics* #1 (1940)

College science geek Jay Garrick becomes the first person to assume the identity of the Flash when he discovers that "hard water vapors" he inhaled while blacked out in his lab have given him the power to move at superhuman speeds. After an abortive stab at a football career, he dons a distinctive winged helmet and red shirt and resolves to fight crime as the Flash.

QUOTE: *"Swifter than the speed of light itself, faster than a bolt of lightning in the sky, is the Flash!"*

JAYNE

ORIGIN: Unknown

SOURCE: *Firefly* (TV series, 2002)

An unusual choice for a boy, but apparently not so on the undisclosed home world of Jayne Cobb, a mercenary who joins forces with Mal Reynolds and his *Serenity* crew on TV's *Firefly*. The impulsive, two-fisted Jayne lives by his own code of honor, though his services are considered negotiable to the highest bidder. He is often the first to warn his crewmates about impending dangers.

QUOTE: *"I'll be in my bunk."*

Jean-Luc

ORIGIN: 24th-century Earth
SOURCE: *Star Trek: The Next Generation* (TV series, 1987–1994)

With his bald pate, distaste for children, and love of "tea, Earl Grey, hot," angular Frenchman Jean-Luc Picard seemed an odd choice for captain of the starship *Enterprise*. But there was a spine of steel backing up that persnickety exterior. The son of a Gallic vintner, this Jean-Luc grows from a youthful hothead (who loses his original heart in a barroom brawl) into a methodical, disciplined man for all seasons—the very model of a starship captain.

QUOTE: *"Make it so."*

Jerome

ORIGIN: Planet Anthea
SOURCE: *The Man Who Fell to Earth* (1976)

Middle name of Thomas Jerome Newton, an alien from the planet Anthea who "falls to Earth" on a mission to secure passage thence for his drought-ravaged people. Gaunt, pasty, and hyper-intelligent, Newton cuts a mysterious, hypnotic figure during his sojourn on our planet. He uses his advanced technological knowledge to amass a large fortune.

QUOTE: *"We'd have probably done the same to you, if you'd come 'round our place."*

Joel

ORIGIN: 20th-century Earth
SOURCE: *Eternal Sunshine of the Spotless Mind* (2004)

Joel is a Hebrew name meaning "God is Lord," a minor Biblical prophet, and the first name of the main character of the 2004 feature *Eternal Sunshine of the Spotless Mind*. Joel Barish is a saturnine loner who briefly finds happiness in the arms of free spirit, Clementine Kruczynski, but elects to have all memory of her erased by a revolutionary scientific procedure when their relationship falls apart.

QUOTE: *"I'm erasing you and I'm happy!"*

Jonas

ORIGIN: Planet Langara
SOURCE: *Stargate SG-1* (TV series, 1997–present)

Autodidact with a photographic memory, Jonas Quinn replaces Daniel Jackson as the resident archaeologist and linguist of Stargate Team 1 on the TV series *Stargate SG-1*. An eager beaver with a zest for new experiences, this Jonas occasionally rubs his fellow crewmembers the wrong way.

QUOTE: *"Politics really do suck wherever you go."*

JONNIE

ORIGIN: Future Earth
SOURCE: *Battlefield Earth* (2000)

Think your little man might have what it takes to save humanity? Then consider naming him after *Battlefield Earth's* cave-dwelling "man-animal" Jonnie Goodboy Tyler, who leaves the safety of his Colorado redoubt to lead the revolution to overthrow Earth's despotic Psychlo overlords in the 2000 space epic.

QUOTE: *"Let it be said that we took this one chance, and fought!"*

JONNY

ORIGIN: 20th-century Earth
SOURCE: *Jonny Quest* (TV series, 1964–1965)

The title character of the animated sci-fi adventure series *Jonny Quest* is a resourceful and quick-witted 13-year-old boy, very much in the mold of his father, Dr. Benton Quest. He also has a strong role model in the form of virile bodyguard Roger "Race" Bannon and a loyal friend in stepbrother Hadji Singh. Jonny is also kind to animals, as evidenced by his love for his dog, Bandit.

QUOTE: *"You were terrific, Race!"*

JUAN

ORIGIN: Egypt, 9th century B.C.E.
SOURCE: *Highlander* (1986)

Juan Sanchez Villa-Lobos Ramirez is an alias adopted by the Egyptian-born Immortal Tak Ne in the 1986 sci-fi fantasy epic *Highlander*. A master swordsman and metallurgist, he takes the sixteenth-century Scottish Immortal Connor MacLeod under his wing, training him in the ways of their kind and preparing him for a climactic battle with the evil Kurgan.

QUOTE: *"There is no substitute for experience."*

JULIUS

ORIGIN: Post-apocalyptic Earth
SOURCE: *Planet of the Apes* (1968)

Sadistic gorilla guard who torments the caged human Taylor with a water hose in *Planet of the Apes*. One of Dr. Zaius's most zealous henchmen in the Ministry of Science, Julius also delights in teasing Taylor about his impending castration.

QUOTE: *"Shut up, you freak!"*

Katsuo

ORIGIN: 20th-century Earth
SOURCE: *Destroy All Monsters* (1968)

Choose this manly Japanese boy's name meaning "victorious child" to honor Katsuo Yamabe, the heroic captain of the interplanetary cruiser SY-3. Katsuo spearheads Earth's defense against the Kilaaks, an alien race bent on siccing the planet's giant monsters on its defenseless cities in the 1968 Japanese beastie bonanza *Destroy All Monsters*.

QUOTE: *"All right, let's go! Time is running out for the human race!"*

Keith

ORIGIN: Unknown
SOURCE: *Voltron: Defender of the Universe* (TV series, 1981–1982)

Commander Keith Kogane leads the Voltron Force, a superteam of space sentinels assigned to protect Planet Arus, on the animated sci-fi TV series *Voltron: Defender of the Universe*. Known for his distinctive red uniform, the thoughtful pilot of the *Black Lion* provides a calming yin to the careening yang of his hotheaded friend and fellow team member, Lance Charles McClain.

QUOTE: *"Form feet and legs; form arms and body; and I'll form the head!"*

Kent

ORIGIN: 20th-century Earth
SOURCE: *The Iron Giant* (1999)

A career in government service may lie in store for the child named after this blustery federal functionary from the 1999 animated feature *The Iron Giant*. A dyed-in-the-wool Cold War stereotype, Kent Mansley leads a campaign to destroy the gentle metallic visitor from another world out of fear he may be a new Soviet secret weapon.

QUOTE: *"A hundred-foot robot? Hee hee. That's nutty."*

KeVin

ORIGIN: 20th-century Earth
SOURCE: *Time Bandits* (1981)

An inquisitive young English boy neglected by his boorish parents, Kevin is finally able to indulge his fascination with history when he is abducted by six time-traveling dwarves and taken on adventures through time in the 1981 fantasy adventure *Time Bandits*.

QUOTE: *"Mom! Dad! It's evil! Don't touch it!"*

OTHER NOTABLE SCI-FI KEVINS: *Kevin Flynn (*Tron *protagonist)*

KiLGore

ORIGIN: 20th-century Earth
SOURCE: *Slaughterhouse-Five* by Kurt Vonnegut (published 1953)

Ilium, New York, native Kilgore Trout, one of the world's most woefully overlooked science-fiction writers, plays important roles in several sci-fi themed novels by Kurt Vonnegut. The author of *Plague on Wheels*, *Oh Say Can You Smell?* and *Maniacs in the Fourth Dimension*, among many other works, he is often published in low-circulation "adult" magazines.

QUOTE: *"We are healthy only to the extent that our ideas are humane."*

KinSaBuro

ORIGIN: 20th-century Earth
SOURCE: *King Kong vs. Godzilla* (1962)

At the behest of his boss, pharmaceutical company drone Kinsaburo Furue travels to Pharoh Island to bring back some mysterious medicinal berries in the 1962 monster fest *King Kong vs. Godzilla*. When his killer corns begin flaring up, he realizes he is in for more than he bargained for.

QUOTE: *"My corns always hurt when they're near a monster."*

KiP

ORIGIN: 20th-century Earth
SOURCE: *Cat Women of the Moon* (1953)

Shoot-from-the-hip copilot Kip Reissner joins mankind's first mission to the moon and finds it inhabited by black-leotard-clad supervixens in the 1953 B-movie *Cat Women of the Moon*. An impulsive man of action who believes in solving problems with a bullet, he is locked in a love triangle with mission leader Laird Grainger and the beautiful Helen Salinger.

QUOTE: *"Believe me, baby, if I ever fell in love with you I'd chase you across the world, around the moon, and all the way stations in between."*

KURt

ORIGIN: 20th-century Earth
SOURCE: *Giant Size X-Men* #1 (Marvel Comics, 1975)

For a touch of the Teutonic, go with this Old German variant of Conrad to honor Kurt Wagner, the elfin, prehensile-tailed X-Man better known as Nightcrawler. A blue-skinned imp endowed with the ability to teleport himself over short distances, this Kurt transcends his slight stature to assume a leadership role within Professor Charles Xavier's mutant superteam.

QUOTE: *"Mein Gott!"*

KYLE

ORIGIN: 20th-century Earth
SOURCE: *Green Lantern* v3 #48 (DC Comics, 1994)

The latest in a long line of men to assume the powers, responsibilities, and tight-fitting emerald bodysuit of the cosmic sentinel called Green Lantern, Kyle Rayner is selected for the post almost at random, after the controversial wig-out of previous Green Lantern Hal Jordan. Like all incarnations of the character, he possesses virtually unlimited control over energy and matter through the use of his power ring.

QUOTE: *"In brightest day, in blackest night, no evil shall escape my sight."*

LANDO

ORIGIN: Unknown
SOURCE: *The Empire Strikes Back* (1980)

A one-time boon companion of Han Solo's, Lando Calrissian is also the former owner of Solo's ship, the *Millennium Falcon*. A roguish smuggler like Solo, the suave, self-interested Lando at first betrays—but later comes to the aid of—his old friend and the rebel cause with which he has aligned himself.

QUOTE: *"The Empire has taken control of this city. I advise every-one to leave before more Imperial troops arrive."*

LENNY

ORIGIN: 20th-century Earth
SOURCE: *Superman IV* (1987)

Lex Luthor's dim-witted nephew Lenny helps him escape from prison in 1987's *Superman IV*, but his usefulness to the criminal mastermind stops there. Though sycophantic and pliable, Lenny is limited by his lack of intellectual candlepower. His first thought when his uncle steals a lock of Superman's hair is to use it to create a "toupee that flies."

QUOTE: *"The Dude of Steel! You are so gonna get it!"*

LEON

ORIGIN: 21st-century Earth
SOURCE: *Blade Runner* (1982)

Last name: Kowalski. Irascible, dull-witted replicant whose artifici-ality is exposed by an LAPD investigator in the opening moments of Ridley Scott's noir sci-fi classic *Blade Runner*. Not as adept at gaming the replicant-detecting Voight-Kampff machine as some of his fellow biorobots, Leon resorts to violence when his identity is uncovered.

QUOTE: *"Wake up. Time to die."*

LESTER

ORIGIN: 20th-century Earth
SOURCE: *Abbott & Costello Go to Mars* (1953)

Gaunt, crabby laborer in a top-secret laboratory who travels to Venus in an experimental rocket ship accidentally launched by his dim-witted buddy Orville in the 1953 sci-fi comedy *Abbott & Costello Go to Mars*.

TRIVIA: *The title* Abbott & Costello Go to Mars *is entirely mislead-ing, since none of the action takes place on the Red Planet.*

VARIANTS: *Les*

LOGAN

ORIGIN: 23rd-century Earth

SOURCE: *Logan's Run* (1976)

"Deep-sleep operative" on a dystopian future Earth who becomes a fugitive after he finds himself targeted for euthanasia as part of a government-run program to stem the tide of overpopulation. (Logan's "run" begins at age twenty-one in the original novel and thirty in the film.) Also known as Logan 5.

QUOTE: *"Life clocks are a lie! Carousel is a lie! There is no renewal!*

LUCAS

ORIGIN: 20th-century Earth

SOURCE: *Uncanny X-Men* #282 (Marvel Comics, 1991)

If you're not using it to honor *Star Wars* creator George, choose this variant form of Luke to recall the heroic contributions of Lucas Bishop, a mutant member of the X-Men blessed with the ability to absorb and redirect energy in the form of powerful concussive blasts.

QUOTE: *"Being an X-Man isn't something you can walk away from."*

LUCIUS

ORIGIN: Post-apocalyptic Earth

SOURCE: *Planet of the Apes* (1968)

Teenage chimpanzee who embodies the rebellious spirit of disenchanted youth on a post-apocalyptic Earth ruled by simians. This nephew of Zira shows courage in helping break the human Taylor out of his cage, but chafes at the lack of respect shown to his generation by its elders.

QUOTE: *"Always giving orders. Just like every other adult!"*

LUKE

ORIGIN: Planet Polis Massa

SOURCE: *Star Wars* (1977)

You'll be paying homage to one of sci-fi lore's most beloved and emulated heroes if you name your boy child after this *Star Wars* protagonist. Raised by his aunt and uncle on the desert planet of Tatooine, Luke Skywalker overcomes his initial reluctance about joining the Rebel Alliance to become a Jedi knight and play a major role in the campaign to overthrow the Galactic Empire and restore the republic. A superb lightsaber duelist with a virtually unrivalled command of the Force, he is the son of Anakin Skywalker (ultimately revealed to be Darth Vader) and brother of Princess Leia.

QUOTE: *"I'm Luke Skywalker. I'm here to rescue you."*

mac

ORIGIN: Unknown
SOURCE: *Earth Girls Are Easy* (1989)

Fuzzy blue space alien made over in the image of Jeff Goldblum in the 1989 sci-fi comedy *Earth Girls Are Easy*. In his humanoid form, Mac wins the heart of a winsome Valley-girl manicurist, Valerie.

QUOTE: *"Are we limp and hard to manage?"*

mace

ORIGIN: Planet Haruun Kal
SOURCE: *Star Wars: The Phantom Menace* (1999)

Legendary Jedi master Mace Windu wields words of wisdom and his trademark purple lightsaber with equal dexterity in the first three episodes of George Lucas's *Star Wars* saga. A philosopher and diplomat on par with Yoda, Mace is one of the first to smell a rat in the form of Chancellor Palpatine, a.k.a. Darth Sidious, by whom he is eventually killed in an epic duel.

QUOTE: *"This party's over."*

malcolm

ORIGIN: 26th-century Shadow
SOURCE: *Firefly* (TV series, 2002)

Malcolm "Mal" Reynolds is the quick-on-the-trigger captain of the *Serenity* on TV's *Firefly*. Fiercely protective of his crew, Mal is a natural-born leader who inspires loyalty and obedience in those who serve under him.

QUOTE: *"We have done the impossible and that makes us mighty."*

manon

ORIGIN: 20th-century Earth
SOURCE: *The Alligator People* (1959)

Crazy, hook-handed Cajun wild man whose pathological hatred of alligators puts him smack in the middle of the action in the 1959

B-movie *The Alligator People*. Having lost a paw to a ravenous gator in his youth, the hard-drinking Manon now brims with bitterness toward the swamp-dwelling creatures, though his rage may also be a by-product of his alcoholism.

QUOTE: *"Dirty, stinkin', slimy gators! You bit my hand off, didn't you? Haha, I'm gonna spend the rest of my life killin' gators. The rest of my life!"*

manuel

ORIGIN: 20th-century Earth
SOURCE: *The Incredible Two-Headed Transplant* (1971)

Homicidal maniac Manuel Cass is less than thrilled to find his sneering head transplanted onto the body of mentally challenged hulk Danny Norton in the 1971 sci-fi shocker *The Incredible Two-Headed Transplant*. He makes the most of his opportunity, however, by asserting his dominance over the weak-willed Danny and leading the two-headed monstrosity on a crime and murder spree.

TRIVIA: *Ads for the film blared: "One Wants to Love, One Wants to Kill!"*

marcus

ORIGIN: Arisia Mining Colony
SOURCE: *Babylon 5* (TV series, 1994–1998)

As the Ranger liaison to the Babylon 5 space station, Marcus Cole is the consummate exemplar of that honorable warrior class, embodying all the chivalric virtues for which they stand. Equal parts swashbuckler and knight errant, he is also known for his charm, wit, and fierce fighting ability.

QUOTE: *"I am a Ranger. We walk in the dark places no others will enter. We stand on the bridge and no one may pass. We live for the One, we die for the One."*

martin

ORIGIN: Planet Mars
SOURCE: *My Favorite Martian* (TV series, 1963–1966)

Name adopted by a Martian stranded on Earth in the 1960s sci-fi sitcom *My Favorite Martian*. "Uncle Martin" lives with genial newspaper reporter Tim O'Hara in suburban Los Angeles, dispensing bon mots, bewildering visitors with his telekinetic powers, and vying for the affection of O'Hara's widowed landlady, Mrs. Lorelei Brown.

QUOTE: *"As a very wise man once told me, the chicken is not infrequently the true dove of peace."*

marty
ORIGIN: 20th-century Earth
SOURCE: *Back to the Future* (1985)
Instill breezy self-confidence in your child, and honor one of the most popular sci-fi comedies of the 1980s, by naming him after Marty McFly, a Reagan-era teenager who tries his rock-and-roll guitar licks out on the uptight 1950s after an eccentric scientist's invention sends him back in time.
QUOTE: *"Are you telling me you built a time machine . . . out of a DeLorean?"*

marvin
ORIGIN: Sirius Cybernetics Corporation
SOURCE: *The Hitchhiker's Guide to the Galaxy* (BBC Radio, 1978)
Morose ship's robot aboard the starship *Heart of Gold* in Douglas Adams's *The Hitchhiker's Guide to the Galaxy*. The so-called Paranoid Android suffers from a debilitating sense of ennui and an unrelentingly downcast view of his existence—in large part because his considerable brainpower is being wasted performing menial tasks aboard Zaphod Beeblebrox's ship.
QUOTE: *"Life! Don't talk to me about life!"*
VARIANTS: *Marv*

miles
ORIGIN: 20th-century Earth
SOURCE: *Invasion of the Body Snatchers* (1956)
Kindly small-town doctor Miles Bennell proves to be mankind's last bulwark against replacement by alien seed pods in the 1956 version of *Invasion of the Body Snatchers*. At first calm and resolute in his struggle against the alien invaders, Miles is eventually reduced to running out in the middle of traffic screaming warnings about the coming takeover.
QUOTE: *"They're here already! You're next!"*
OTHER NOTABLE SCI-FI MILES: *Miles Monroe (cryogenically frozen nebbish,* Sleeper*), Miles O'Brien (transporter chief,* Star Trek: The Next Generation *and* Star Trek: Deep Space Nine*)*

morgan

ORIGIN: 20th-century Earth
SOURCE: *Food of the Gods* (1975)

Environmentally conscious professional football player whose hunting weekend on a remote Canadian island is disrupted by the emergence of giant mutated wasps, chickens, and rats in the 1975 film *Food of the Gods*, "based on a portion of the novel by H. G. Wells."

QUOTE: *"One of these days the earth will get even with man for messing her up with his garbage."*

morpheus

ORIGIN: 22nd-century Earth
SOURCE: *The Matrix* (1999)

Oracular hovercraft captain (named for the god of dreams in Greek mythology) and itinerant rebel wrangler, one of the leaders of the struggle to overthrow the machine masters who enslave future Earth. Known for his opaque pronouncements, effortless cool, and enviable taste in sunglasses.

QUOTE: *"No one can be told what the Matrix is. You have to see it for yourself."*

nat

ORIGIN: 20th-century Earth
SOURCE: *The Astounding She-Monster* (1957)

Short form of Nathaniel preferred by Nat Burdell, a dapper but dull-witted thug whose abduction of a wealthy heiress is complicated by the appearance of a sexy blonde radioactive alien in the 1957 B-movie *The Astounding She-Monster*.

QUOTE: *"The way you keep puttin' your foot in your kisser, it's a wonder you don't get athlete's mouth!"*

nestor

ORIGIN: Nestor Consciousness
SOURCE: *Battle Beyond the Stars* (1980)

This Greek name meaning "traveler" can recall a brave old king from Homer's *Iliad*, Hall of Fame baseball umpire Nestor Chylak, or, for sci-fi fans, a race of highly evolved hive-minded beings who help the beleaguered people of Akir liberate themselves from the evil Sador in the 1980 B-movie space opera *Battle Beyond the Stars*.

QUOTE: *"There is only one Nestor, one consciousness. As you might imagine, this has proven very lonely and very dull."*

Orin

ORIGIN: Atlantis
SOURCE: *More Fun Comics* #73 (1941)

To instill a reverence for the sea in your child, consider the name given at birth to the "Sea King" himself, DC Comics' underwater superhero Aquaman. This son of the Queen of Atlantis and a mysterious wizard is abandoned to the world of humans as a child, but spends the rest of his life yearning to return to the ocean. His telepathic dominion over sea creatures is formidable.

TRIVIA: *Aquaman's adopted human name is Arthur Curry.*

Orville

ORIGIN: 20th-century Earth
SOURCE: *Abbott & Costello Go to Mars* (1953)

Sure, you could name your son Orville after Orville Wright, one of the pioneers of flight. But just remember you'll also be saddling him with the name of Orville, the bumbling buffoon who accidentally launches an experimental rocket ship that sends him and his buddy Lester on a trip to Venus in the 1953 sci-fi comedy *Abbott & Costello Go to Mars*.

TRIVIA: *Abbott and Costello's only foray into sci-fi is widely considered the duo's worst film.*

Oscar

ORIGIN: 20th-century Earth
SOURCE: *The Six Million Dollar Man* (TV series, 1974–1978)

A career in espionage may await the child named after Oscar Goldman, the chief of the Office of Scientific Intelligence (OSI) in charge of the bionic human program on *The Six Million Dollar Man* and *The Bionic Woman*. Dapper, with a fondness for loud, wide ties, the resourceful, toupeed Goldman travels around with spare bionic parts in his briefcase, always ready to lend a hand—or eyeball—to Steve Austin and Jaime Sommers.

QUOTE: *"We can rebuild him."*

PaVeL

ORIGIN: 23rd-century Earth
SOURCE: *Star Trek* (TV series, 1966–1969)

This Russian form of the name Paul pays tribute to Pavel Andreievich Chekov, the brash, Beatle-coiffed navigator of the starship *Enterprise*. An only child, Chekov takes great pride in his ethnic heritage, often regaling his crewmates with boasts about Russian scientific and technological accomplishments.

QUOTE: *"Excuse me, I'm looking for nuclear wessels."*

PHiLiP

ORIGIN: 20th-century Earth
SOURCE: *Futurama* (TV series, 1999–2003)

Pizza delivery man Philip J. Fry enters cryogenic freeze on New Year's Eve 1999 and wakes up a thousand years later in the sci-fi comedy cartoon series *Futurama*. A dogged optimist, Philip has a kind heart and enterprising spirit. He makes the best of his time-traveling experience by applying his twentieth-century skill set to his new job as a deliveryman for Planet Express.

QUOTE: *"You can't give up hope just because it's hopeless. You gotta hope even more, and cover your ears and go 'bla bla bla bla bla bla bla bla!'"*

PiOtr

ORIGIN: 20th-century Earth
SOURCE: *Giant Size X-Men* #1 (Marvel Comics, 1975)

Russian form of Peter made famous by Piotr Nikolaievitch Rasputin, a Russian mutant better known as the X-Men member Colossus. Raised on a Soviet collective farm, young Piotr is recruited by Professor Charles Xavier to join his new X team after word gets out about his uncanny ability to transform his entire body into organic steel at will. A gentle giant with an artistic temperament, Piotr only reluctantly signs on with the X-Men out of concern for the betterment of mankind.

QUOTE: *"Boszhe Moi!"*

Race

ORIGIN: 20th-century Earth
SOURCE: *Jonny Quest* (TV series, 1964–1965)

Roger "Race" Bannon is the intrepid family bodyguard on the animated sci-fi adventure series *Jonny Quest*. The consummate man of action, Race repeatedly lays his life on the line to protect Jonny, Dr. Benton Quest, Hadji Singh, and their companion animal, Bandit the Dog. He appears to suffer from a form of albinism.

QUOTE: *"Hey, I was only doin' my job!"*

RACK

ORIGIN: 20th-century Earth
SOURCE: *Kingdom of the Spiders* (1977)

Studly nickname used by Robert Hansen, the laconic Arizona veterinarian played by William Shatner in 1977's *Kingdom of the Spiders*. An avid outdoorsman and ladies' man, the respected animal sawbones fights back manfully as his small town is overrun by rampaging mutant tarantulas. His nickname derives from childhood billiard-playing experiences.

QUOTE: *"Buckle up for safety, honey."*

RANDALL

ORIGIN: Unknown
SOURCE: *Time Bandits* (1981)

Name your little man after one of sci-fi cinema's most beloved little persons, the ringleader of a troupe of six time-traveling dwarves who abduct a young English boy and take him on amazing adventures through history in the 1981 fantasy adventure *Time Bandits*.

QUOTE: *"You see, to be quite frank, Kevin, the fabric of the universe is far from perfect. It was a bit of botched job, you see. We only had seven days to make it."*

RAY

ORIGIN: 20th-century Earth
SOURCE: *The War of the Worlds* (2005)

New Jersey dockworker Ray Ferris finds himself swept up in the invasion of Earth by murderous tripods from Mars in the 2005 film version of H. G. Wells's *The War of the Worlds*. On the up side, the catastrophe gives him a great opportunity to mend fences with his estranged family, whom he must repeatedly rescue from alien annihilation.

QUOTE: *"I am not going to let my daughter die because of you!"*

OTHER NOTABLE SCI-FI RAYS: *Ray Erikson* (Mansquito, *the infamous Sci-Fi Channel TV movie*)

REGINALD

ORIGIN: 24th-century Earth
SOURCE: *Star Trek: The Next Generation* (TV series, 1987–1994)

Old English for "counsel power," this no-longer-fashionable boy's name honors Reginald Barclay, the USS *Enterprise's* timorous, fearful diagnostic engineer. Shy and stammering, Barclay suffers from multiple phobias, including social anxiety, an irrational dread of the transporter, and an aversion to spiders.

QUOTE: *"I am the guy who writes down things to remember to say when there's a party. And then when he finally gets there, he winds up alone in the corner trying to look comfortable examining a potted plant."*

ROGER

ORIGIN: 21st-century Earth
SOURCE: *Star Crystal* (1986)

Civilian computer engineer aboard the NASA space shuttle SC37 who encounters a ravenous alien life form named Gar in the low-budget 1986 sci-fi shocker *Star Crystal*.

QUOTE: *"We civilians, unlike you military personnel, do it right the first time."*

ROJ

ORIGIN: Future Earth
SOURCE: *Blake's Seven* (BBC TV series, 1978–1981)

Intergalactic freedom fighter Roj Blake leads a ragtag band of revolutionaries on a quest to overthrow the oppressive galactic government known as the Federation in the BBC sci-fi series *Blake's Seven*. While initially principled and driven, the intense, tightly permed Blake grows increasingly fanatical as his seditious activities take an ever greater human toll.

QUOTE: *"You can't separate living creatures. Being alive involves them together."*

ROY

ORIGIN: 20th-century Earth
SOURCE: *Close Encounters of the Third Kind* (1977)

Last name: Neary. Affable electric lineman who has a "close encounter" with aliens in the cab of his truck while investigating a mysterious power outage in *Close Encounters of the Third Kind*.

Transformed by his experience, this unassuming family man is haunted by visions of Devil's Tower National Monument (at one point fashioning a replica of it out of mashed potatoes). He eventually travels there with other pilgrims seeking communion with the extraterrestrial mothership.

QUOTE: *"Dammit! I know this. I know what this is! This means something!"*

OTHER NOTABLE SCI-FI ROYS: *Roy Batty (replicant ringleader, Blade Runner)*

RUFUS

ORIGIN: Future Earth
SOURCE: *Bill and Ted's Excellent Adventure* (1989)
Guitar-strumming wise man from the future who lends his time machine to two teenage buffoons in an effort to help them pass their history test in the 1989 sci-fi themed comedy *Bill and Ted's Excellent Adventure.*

QUOTE: *"Gentlemen . . . we're history."*

RUSSELL

ORIGIN: 20th-century Earth
SOURCE: *Independence Day* (1996)
Alcoholic crop duster who sacrifices himself to rescue the world from alien invasion in 1996's *Independence Day.* A decorated air force veteran turned burned-out single father, brash, defiant Russell Casse is driven by grief over his wife's death and anger over his alleged alien abduction several years earlier. He flies his jet into the heart of the alien ship, destroying it and saving humanity.

QUOTE: *"In the words of my generation: Up yours!"*

SEAN

ORIGIN: 20th-century Earth
SOURCE: *Giant Size X-Men* #1 (Marvel Comics, 1975)
Sure, you can choose this popular Irish variant of John to honor Scotsman Sean Connery of *Zardoz* fame, but to show the green along with your sci-fi savvy you'll choose it to honor Sean Cassidy, the Irish-born X-Man better known as Banshee. Heir to a fortune back in Erin, this Sean forsakes a life of leisure to put his powerful "sonic scream" to use fighting evil mutants and other threats

to humanity.

TRIVIA: *Although Banshee is male, in Irish mythology banshees are always female.*

VARIANT: *Shawn*

SHERMAN

ORIGIN: 20th-century Earth
SOURCE: *TerrorVision* (1986)

Last name: Putterman. Fearful, prescription-pill-popping tyke who discovers that his dysfunctional family's satellite dish has become the conduit for an alien from the planet Pluton in the low-budget 1986 feature *TerrorVision*. When his warnings are dismissed by his elders, the resourceful Sherman at first tries to kill the murderous monster, but ultimately opts to befriend the creature instead.

QUOTE: *"Hello? This is Sherman again. There's really a monster. It's eating Mom and Dad."*

SIMON

ORIGIN: Unknown
SOURCE: *Starcrash* (1979)

This swashbuckling Luke Skywalker analog from the 1979 Italian-made *Star Wars* knockoff *Starcrash* possesses his forebear's amazing ability with a lightsaber, but with bigger hair and less moon-eyed mysticism. There's also the added appeal of knowing you named your son after one of the first characters ever played by David Hasselhoff.

QUOTE: *"The Emperor will make you pay for this!"*

SNAKE

ORIGIN: 20th-century Earth
SOURCE: *Escape from New York* (1981)

It'll take guts to name your son after Snake Plissken, the one-eyed convict sent to rescue the captive president of the United States from the maximum-security hellhole that is 1997 Manhattan in *Escape from New York*. But at least you'll have the comfort of knowing he'll have the fortitude to extricate himself from seemingly impossible situations.

QUOTE: *"Call me Snake."*

SOL

ORIGIN: 21st-century Earth
SOURCE: *Soylent Green* (1973)

Last name: Roth. Aging, liverspotted resident of Earth's overpopulated future who longs for the good old days when you could get real food instead of artificial foodstuffs. Disgusted with the state of society, Sol opts to be euthanized in an antiseptic "suicide parlor" rather than go on living in a world without lamb shanks.

QUOTE: *"When I was a kid, you could buy meat anywhere! Eggs they had, real butter! Not this crap!"*

TAFFY

ORIGIN: 21st-century Earth
SOURCE: *Blade Runner* (1982)

Taffy Lewis is a seedy saloonkeeper in the dystopian future Los Angeles depicted in *Blade Runner*. His eponymous establishment is frequented by replicants and the blade runners charged with hunting down and terminating them. Taffy does not cooperate with the LAPD, preferring to shoo them away with free drinks.

QUOTE: *"Hey Louie, the man is dry. Give him one on the house."*

THADDEUS

ORIGIN: Unknown
SOURCE: *Space Ghost and Dino Boy* (TV series, 1966–1968)

Thaddeus Bach is the real name of the intergalactic crime fighter known as Space Ghost. Endowed with the power to fly and shoot beams from his eyes and wrist-mounted power bands, the black-cowled wraith patrols the galaxy accompanied by his cohorts Jan, Jace, and Blip the Monkey.

QUOTE: *"Let's see how they like my energy ray!"*

TIBERIUS

ORIGIN: 23rd-century Earth
SOURCE: *Star Trek* (TV series, 1966–1969)

This ancient Roman name (for the river on which the city of Rome was founded), bestowed upon the second emperor of the Julio-Claudian line, also honors the middle name of the starship *Enterprise*'s intrepid captain. Tiberius only reluctantly accepted the imperial throne at the urging of his mother, Livia. The impulsive

James Tiberius Kirk bears none of his namesake's saturnine disposition, however. See also Kirk (p. 153).

TRIVIA: In the first-season Star Trek *episode "Where No Man Has Gone Before," Kirk's middle initial is erroneously given as "R."*

TOSHiO

ORIGIN: 20th-century Earth
SOURCE: *Gamera* (1965)

A career in herpetology may await the son named after this naïve, trusting Japanese boy who bonds with the enormous fire-breathing title turtle in 1965's *Gamera.*

QUOTE: "Gamera saved my life for me once. Gamera's really a nice turtle."

TRAViS

ORIGIN: 22nd-century Earth
SOURCE: *Star Trek: Enterprise* (TV series, 2001–2005)

Travis Mayweather is the helmsman aboard the USS *Enterprise* under its first commander, Captain Jonathan Archer. Having lived his entire life in space, the energetic, enthusiastic Travis is one of the most talented pilots in Starfleet and a knowledgeable guide to planetary hot spots.

QUOTE: "One thing I can tell you is that at warp one point eight, you've got a lot of time on your hands between ports. That's how my parents wound up with me."

TRUMAN

ORIGIN: 20th-century Earth
SOURCE: *The Truman Show* (1998)

A career as a reality TV star may await the child named after Truman Burbank, the unwitting lead player in a long-running television program in the 1998 feature *The Truman Show.* This name is actually rife with hidden meanings; it could stand for "true man" or "Totally Recorded hUMAN life," while Truman's last name, Burbank, is a city in southern California where many television shows are filmed.

QUOTE: "Somebody help me, I'm being spontaneous!"

TUCK

ORIGIN: 20th-century Earth
SOURCE: *Innerspace* (1987)

In the 1987 sci-fi comedy *Innerspace*, Tuck Pendleton is a cocksure test pilot who volunteers to be miniaturized and injected into a lab rabbit as part of a top-secret experiment. Comic complications ensue when the syringe containing Tuck is mistakenly plunged into the buttocks of a neurotic supermarket clerk played by Martin Short.

QUOTE: *"When things are at their darkest, pal, it's a brave man that can kick back and party."*

VINCE

ORIGIN: 20th-century Earth
SOURCE: *The Green Slime* (1968)

Short form of Vincent preferred by hotheaded space station commander Vince Elliott in the 1968 sci-fi oozefest *The Green Slime*. Embittered at being relieved of command by his professional and romantic rival Jack Rankin, Vince finds a measure of redemption in a heroic but suicidal attempt to destroy the repulsive slime entity.

QUOTE: *"Now since that's the way it is let's be sure that's the way it is, huh?"*

VIRGIL

ORIGIN: 20th-century Earth
SOURCE: *Battle for the Planet of the Apes* (1973)

Diminutive ape elder who counsels Caesar with quotations from simian scripture in 1973's *Battle for the Planet of the Apes*. A thoughtful, soft-spoken orangutan, Virgil is an eloquent advocate of peaceful coexistence with humans.

QUOTE: *"Ape shall not kill ape."*

WALLY

ORIGIN: 20th-century Earth
SOURCE: *The Flash* #110 (DC Comics, 1959)

Short form of Wallace preferred by Wally West, nephew and protégé of Barry Allen, and the third man to don the scarlet togs of the superfast superhero known as the Flash. Originally known as Kid Flash, Wally assumes the Flash mantle in the wake of his uncle's heroic death.

QUOTE: *"My name is Wally West, and I'm the fastest man alive."*

WALTER

ORIGIN: Planet Antarea
SOURCE: *Cocoon* (1985)

Old-school human name assumed by an alien from the planet Antarea who comes to Earth to retrieve some lost comrades but ends up bonding with the aged denizens of a Florida retirement community in the heartwarming 1985 sci-fi feature *Cocoon*.

QUOTE: *"Every 10 or 11,000 years I make a horrible mistake."*

WARREN

ORIGIN: 23rd-century Earth
SOURCE: *Babylon 5* (TV series, 1994–1998)

Last name: Keffer. This handsome, cocksure Starfury pilot in Babylon 5's Zeta squadron brings *Top Gun*–style brashness to the space station's defense and peacekeeping operations. While dismissed by many as a shallow hotshot, Warren's poetic side emerges in his eloquent description of a Shadow ship.

QUOTE: *"It was jet black, a shade of black so deep your eye just kind of slides off it. And it shimmered when you looked at it. A spider, big as death and twice as ugly. And when it flies past, it's like you hear a scream in your mind."*

OTHER NOTABLE SCI-FI WARRENS: *Warren Worthington (X-Man Archangel)*

WESLEY

ORIGIN: 24th-century Earth
SOURCE: *Star Trek: The Next Generation* (TV series, 1987–1994)

Choose this Old English place name meaning "western meadow" if you want your son to be a precocious teen prodigy like Ensign Wesley Crusher of the starship *Enterprise*-D. The son of a medical officer and a ship's second officer tragically killed in the line of duty, the ever-resourceful Wesley repeatedly saves the ship from destruction, often using jerry-rigged science experiments.

TRIVIA: *Wesley is also the middle name of* Star Trek *creator Gene Roddenberry.*

WiLLiE

ORIGIN: 20th-century Earth
SOURCE: *ALF* (TV series. 1986–1990)

Beleaguered householder Willie Tanner struggles to adjust to life with an alien houseguest on the sci-fi sitcom *ALF*. A doting father and loving husband, the agreeable Willie finds his patience repeatedly tested by "Alien Life Form" Gordon Shumway's knavish capering.

QUOTE: *"ALF, while we're gone, I trust you won't be getting into any mischief."*

Winston

ORIGIN: 20th-century Oceania
SOURCE: *1984* by George Orwell (published 1949)

Recalcitrant clerk for the Ministry of Truth in the nightmarish police state of Oceania in George Orwell's *1984*. An independent thinker who is rebellious by nature, Winston chafes against his repressive milieu, engaging in small acts of sabotage and vandalism and later attempting to join the anti-Statist resistance.

QUOTE: *"How can I help seeing what is in front of my eyes? Two and two are four."*

Zac

ORIGIN: Caprica Colony
SOURCE: *Battlestar Galactica* (1978)

The beloved son of Commander Adama in the 1978 film version of *Battlestar Galactica*, Zac is tragically killed in a Cylon sneak attack. His death provides personal motivation for Adama and his surviving son, Apollo, in their fight against the Cylons.

TRIVIA: *In the 2004–present* Battlestar Galactica *TV series, Zac is spelled Zack.*

Zachary

ORIGIN: 20th-century Earth
SOURCE: *Lost in Space* (TV series, 1965–1968)

Dithering saboteur Dr. Zachary Smith finds himself "lost in space" with the Robinson family and their ambulatory robot after he stows away aboard their ship in this popular 1960s sci-fi series. A dyspeptic fussbudget who cares little for his companions' safety, Smith works feverishly to get himself rescued when not pursuing his passions for opera, chess, gardening, gourmet food, and wine.

QUOTE: *"Oh, the pain, the pain!"*

zack

ORIGIN: 23rd-century Earth
SOURCE: *Babylon 5* (TV series, 1994–1998)

Earnest, trustworthy Zack Allan succeeds Michael Garibaldi as chief of security on space station Babylon 5. No stereotypical rent-a-cop, this Zack is known to be conscientious, loyal, and "by the book." In fact, he feels guilty about ascending to Garibaldi's former position.

QUOTE: *"I don't believe in random attacks. Maybe there's not an obvious reason, but there's always a reason."*

CHAPTER 3
FEMININE NAMES

This one's for the ladies. For far too long, sci-fi lore has relegated women to the stereotypical roles of screaming victim and alien supervixen. In recent years, however, more interesting and nuanced characters have finally emerged. Choose your little girl's name from this smorgasbord of space monarchs, karate-chopping supermoms, and interstellar adventuresses.

AERYN

ORIGIN: Unknown
SOURCE: *Farscape* (TV series, 1999–2003)

This distinctive variant form of Erin honors the butt-kicking commando Aeryn Sun, a Sebacean, born and bred into a militaristic mindset, who struggles to transcend her conditioning and find nonviolent means to solve problems during her sojourn on the living Leviathan ship *Moya*. Aggressive by nature, Aeryn is a crack pilot and master of hand-to-hand and weapons combat.

QUOTE: *"No offense, human, but what could I possibly need from you?"*

ALEX

ORIGIN: Future Earth
SOURCE: *Saturn 3* (1980)

Eye-popping assistant in an outer space food research station played by 1970s pinup queen Farrah Fawcett in the 1980 film *Saturn 3*. Alex lives in a state of bliss with the only other inhabitant of Saturn 3—the geriatric Major Adam—until their idyllic routine of running tests, making love, and taking showers together is interrupted by the arrival of the homicidal Captain Benson and his menacing robot, Hector.

QUOTE: *"I'm with the major."*

ALICE

ORIGIN: 21st-century Earth
SOURCE: *Resident Evil* (2001)

Alice is the fearless, kick-butt heroine of the *Resident Evil* videogame/movie franchise. An amnesiac employee of the sinister, hydralike Umbrella Corporation, Alice may take her name from the title character of Lewis Carroll's *Alice's Adventures in Wonderland*.

QUOTE: *"I'm not dead yet."*

ALLURA

ORIGIN: Planet Venus
SOURCE: *Abbott & Costello Go to Mars* (1953)

Venusian queen who chooses Lou Costello's clownish Earth man Orville as her consort in the 1952 sci-fi comedy *Abbott & Costello Go to Mars*.

FEMININE NAMES

TRIVIA: *All the Venusian women in* Abbott & Costello Go to Mars *were played by real-life beauty-pageant winners.*

AMY

ORIGIN: 30th-Century Mars
SOURCE: *Futurama* (TV series, 1999–2003)
From the Old French for "beloved," Amy is an increasingly popular girl's name and looks likely to remain so well into the future—witness Amy Wong, the scatterbrained engineering student who interns with Professor Hugo Farnsworth at Planet Express on the sci-fi cartoon series *Futurama*.
QUOTE: *"Hey, let's go car shopping! My parents said if I got all Bs they'd buy me a bar. And I got all Cs!"*

ANN

ORIGIN: 20th-century Earth
SOURCE: *The Killer Shrews* (1959)
Attractive blonde zoologist Ann Craigis accompanies her father, the legendary Swedish scientist Marlow Craigis, to an isolated island, where the side effects of his experiments with human miniaturization have resulted in the proliferation of dozens of giant mutated shrews in the 1959 B-movie *The Killer Shrews*.
QUOTE: *"The wind has a lonesome sound, doesn't it?"*
VARIANTS: *Ana, Anna, Anne*

BRENDA

ORIGIN: 20th-century Earth
SOURCE: *Highlander* (1986)
Police forensic scientist Brenda Wyatt leads the investigation into a series of mysterious decapitation murders in the 1986 sci-fi fantasy epic *Highlander*. She eventually falls for her prime suspect, Connor McLeod, an Immortal from sixteenth-century Scotland, learns his true nature, and becomes his wife. Fittingly, her name is Old Norse for "sword" and is quite common in Scotland.
QUOTE: *"What can you tell me about a seven-foot lunatic hacking away at a broadsword at one o'clock in the morning, New York City, 1985?"*

Brooke

ORIGIN: 20th-century Earth
SOURCE: *Manimal* (TV series, 1983)

Fetching police detective Brooke McKenzie accidentally discovers the shape-shifting secret identity of the TV superhero known as Manimal on the eponymous 1980s sci-fi adventure series. Though taken in by his animal magnetism, Brooke keeps their collaboration within professional bounds—helping Manimal solve crimes and, presumably, cleaning up whatever messes he leaves behind.

TRIVIA: *Actress Melody Anderson, who played Brooke, previously played Dale Arden in the 1980 film version of* Flash Gordon.

Carla

ORIGIN: 19th-century Earth
SOURCE: *Journey to the Center of the Earth* (1959)

With the persistence of a true adventurer, strong-willed widow Carla Goetaborg invites herself along on Professor Oliver Lindenbrook's expedition to Earth's molten core in the 1959 sci-fi adventure *Journey to the Center of the Earth.*

TRIVIA: *Carla's improbable surname was inspired by the name of Sweden's second-largest city, Göteborg.*

Claire

ORIGIN: 20th-century Earth
SOURCE: *It Conquered the World* (1956)

Devoted wife Claire Anderson desperately tries to save her scientist husband from the thrall of a manipulative Venusian with whom he's been communicating in the low-budget 1956 alien invasion feature *It Conquered the World.*

QUOTE: *"You can't rub the tarnish from men's souls without losing a little of the silver, too."*

Clementine

ORIGIN: 20th-century Earth
SOURCE: *Eternal Sunshine of the Spotless Mind* (2004)

Choose this name to commemorate your favorite type of orange, the drowned subject of a popular folk ballad, or Clementine Kruczynski, the free-spirited, memory-erasing heroine of the 2004 feature *Eternal Sunshine of the Spotless Mind.*

QUOTE: *"Look, I'm sorry if I came off a little nutso. I'm not really."*

CONSUELLA

ORIGIN: Post-apocalyptic Earth
SOURCE: *Zardoz* (1974)

Ravishing Vortex-dwelling "Eternal" with a professed fascination for the mechanics of the male genitalia in the 1974 gonzo sci-fi epic *Zardoz*. While repulsed by carnality, she finds herself drawn to the brutish Zed, despite her fears that he will contaminate the Eternal community.

QUOTE: *"These images will pollute us."*

CORA

ORIGIN: 20th-century Earth
SOURCE: *Fantastic Voyage* (1966)

A career on the frontiers of medicine may await the girl named after scientist's assistant Cora Peterson, one of five people miniaturized and sent into the bloodstream of a Czech defector in an effort to remove a life-threatening blood clot from his brain in the 1966 feature *Fantastic Voyage*.

QUOTE: *"We're going to see things no one has ever seen before. Just think about it."*

DALE

ORIGIN: 20th-century Earth
SOURCE: *Flash Gordon* comic strip (1934)

Danger-prone Dale Arden accompanies interstellar adventurer Flash Gordon on his journey to planet Mongo in Dr. Hans Zarkov's rocket ship. As Flash's main squeeze, her role is largely limited to screaming, becoming imperiled, and serving as arm candy for the strapping space-age hero.

QUOTE: *"Oh, Flash!"*

DEANNA

ORIGIN: Planet Betazed
SOURCE: *Star Trek: The Next Generation* (TV series, 1987–1994)

This feminine form of Dean (Old English for "valley") also evokes Deanna Troi, the half-human, half-Betazoid ship's counselor aboard the USS *Enterprise*-D. Gifted with the empathic ability to sense the emotions of other beings, Deanna is a superb listener, keenly attuned to the problems of those around her—the consummate other-directed individual.

QUOTE: *"There is something to be learned when you're not in control of every situation."*

DEBBIE

ORIGIN: 20th-century Earth
SOURCE: *Killer Klowns from Outer Space* (1988)

Diminutive form of Deborah used by small-town resident Debbie Stone in the low-budget 1988 alien invasion feature *Killer Klowns from Outer Space*. She is among the first to encounter the aliens dressed as circus clowns and is briefly imprisoned by them in a hot air balloon.

QUOTE: *"I don't believe in UFOs, but if they do exist, then we're trapped in one right now."*

DEVON

ORIGIN: 22nd-century Earth
SOURCE: *Earth 2* (TV series, 1994)

The archetypal strong-willed, protective, butt-kicking sci-fi female, wealthy architect and single mother Devon Adair courageously leads an expedition to a supposedly uninhabitable planet in an effort to find a cure for her son's mysterious disease in the short-lived TV series *Earth 2*.

QUOTE: *"We came to this planet a group of strangers. And now we head out, still strangers, but united toward a single purpose."*

DIANA

ORIGIN: Ancient Greece
SOURCE: *All-Star Comics* #8 (All-American Publications, 1941)

Multiple-superpowered princess of the Amazons, sent by the goddess Aphrodite to twentieth-century Earth to help mankind battle the Nazis using the sobriquet Wonder Woman. Armed with her magic lasso (and assisted by boyfriend Steve Trevor) Wonder Woman is the personification of female power and ability.

QUOTE: *"If we can't believe in a higher law than that of man . . . if the bond between mother and child is worthless—what are we fighting for?"*

VARIANTS: *Diane*

DODO

ORIGIN: 20th-century Earth
SOURCE: *Dr. Who* (BBC TV series, 1963–present)
Short form of Dorothea used by an orphaned Cockney waif who accompanies the first incarnation of the Time Lord known as the Doctor on his travels through time and space. Dodo Chaplet has a humane, caring nature, with an independent streak and a strong sense of fair play.
QUOTE: *"Wait a minute, if this isn't a police box, what is it? And who are you?"*

ELEANOR

ORIGIN: 20th-century Earth
SOURCE: *V* (TV series, 1983)
If you're looking to raise a rebel, you may want to steer clear of this old-fashioned derivative of Helen. Sure, Eleanor Roosevelt rattled a few cages in her day, but on the TV series *V* Eleanor Dupres is one of the most abject collaborators with the alien invasion force known as the Visitors.
QUOTE: *"I know the Visitors aren't saints. But they're in power! They are power."*

ELISABETH

ORIGIN: 20th-century Earth
SOURCE: *New Mutants Annual* #2 (Marvel Comics, 1986)
Little-used variant form of Elizabeth used by Elisabeth Braddock, an English-born mutant with telekinetic and precognitive abilities who joins the X-Men as Psylocke.
TRIVIA: *Elisabeth Braddock is the twin sister of Brian Braddock, a.k.a. Captain Britain.*

ELLA

ORIGIN: 21st-century Earth
SOURCE: *Rollerball* (1975)
If a career in the corporate world is what you seek for your daughter, consider this name from *Rollerball*, which evokes Ella, the beloved wife of Rollerball superstar Jonathan E. Taken from her husband and betrothed to a high-ranking Energy Corporation official, she eventually returns at the behest of her company bosses to convince Jonathan to quit the deadly sport so that his martyr-

dom does not stir a revival of the spirit of individuality in the lethargic populace.

QUOTE: *"Comfort is freedom. It always has been."*

ELLIE

ORIGIN: 20th-century Earth
SOURCE: *Jurassic Park* (1993)

Paleontology graduate student Ellie Sattler joins her professor Dr. Alan Grant on an ill-fated tour of a dinosaur theme park in the 1993 sci-fi monster mash-up *Jurassic Park*. This short form of Ella or Eleanor has exploded in popularity in recent decades and currently ranks in the top two hundred most-popular girl's names.

QUOTE: *"We can discuss 'sexism in survival situations' when I get back."*

OTHER NOTABLE SCI-FI ELLIES: *Ellie Arroway (extraterrestrial-seeking scientist,* Contact*)*

ESMERALIDA

ORIGIN: Planet Jillucia
SOURCE: *Message from Space* (1978)

If you've already used "Leia" and want to continue the theme, consider naming your second daughter after this Princess Leia analog from the 1978 Japanese *Star Wars* knock-off *Message from Space*. Princess Esmeralida is an emissary from the peaceful planet Jillucia seeking warriors to defend it from invasion by the evil Gavanas empire.

QUOTE: *"Surrender? We Jillucians do not surrender! Get this into your head: Jillucians are not your cattle."*

EVEY

ORIGIN: 20th-century Earth
SOURCE: *V for Vendetta* (DC Comics, 1992)

Evey Hammond is the main character in the comic book series and feature film *V for Vendetta*, created by Alan Moore. A teenage waif in a dystopian London ruled by an authoritarian government, she comes under the wing of the mysterious masked revolutionary known as V and eventually becomes his successor. Her name seems to presage this transformation—deriving as it does from the letters *E* (the fifth letter of the alphabet, five being V in Roman numerals) and *V.*

QUOTE: *"This country needs more than a building right now. It needs hope."*

Ezri

ORIGIN: Planet New Sydney
SOURCE: *Star Trek: Deep Space Nine* (TV series, 1993–1999)

Ezri Dax is a Trill ensign who inherits the Dax symbiont from Jadzia Dax on TV's *Star Trek: Deep Space Nine*. A reluctant host, Ezri Dax has trouble integrating the experiences of the previous Dax hosts and relating to some members of the grieving Deep Space Nine crew—particularly Jadzia Dax's widower, Worf.

QUOTE: *"It's a strange sensation, dying. No matter how many times it happens to you, you never get used to it."*

Gerry

ORIGIN: 20th-century Earth
SOURCE: *Night of the Lepus* (1972)

Arizona entomologist Gerry Bennett and her husband, Roy, inadvertently trigger an invasion by hordes of man-eating mutant rabbits when their daughter adopts a bunny dosed with an experimental DNA-altering serum in the alarmist 1972 animal attack shocker *Night of the Lepus*.

QUOTE: *"Rabbits aren't exactly Roy's bag!"*

Gertie

ORIGIN: 20th-century Earth
SOURCE: *E.T. The Extraterrestrial* (1982)

Short form of Gertrude (Old German for "strength of a spear") used for Elliott's younger sister in *E.T. The Extraterrestrial*. (No last name is given for any of the characters.) Together with Elliott and their older brother, Michael, adorable Gertie helps shelter the stranded alien botanist from the authorities.

QUOTE: *"Alligators in the sewers."*

Grace

ORIGIN: 21st-century Earth
SOURCE: *Death Race 2000* (1975)

This regal, classic girl's name evokes both screen icon Grace Kelly and Grace Pander, the disturbingly cheerful telejournalist who conducts live TV interviews with the widows of drivers killed in the hellish transcontinental road race known as Death Race 2000.

QUOTE: *"She was a great, dear friend of mine, and I shall remember her forever howling down that freeway in the sky, knocking over . . . the angels."*

GWEN

ORIGIN: 20th-century Earth
SOURCE: *Amazing Spider-Man* #31 (Marvel Comics, 1965)

Gwendolyn "Gwen" Stacy is Mary Jane Watson's blonde-haired rival for the teenage affections of Peter Parker (a.k.a. Spider-Man). As Peter's first love, the beautiful, bubbly Gwen will always have a special place in his heart, but she meets with a tragic end when she is dropped off a bridge and murdered by Spider-Man's arch-nemesis, the Green Goblin.

QUOTE: *"Peter Parker is the only boy I've met who hasn't given me a tumble!"*

HELEN

ORIGIN: 20th-century Earth
SOURCE: *Cat Women of the Moon* (1953)

In the 1953 B-movie *Cat Women of the Moon*, Helen Salinger is the multitalented mission navigator on mankind's first expedition to the moon—although she must convince her male colleagues to take her along with boasts about her cooking prowess.

QUOTE: *"Someone's got to cook your meals for you!"*

HELENE

ORIGIN: 20th-century Earth
SOURCE: *The Fly* (1958)

As the long-suffering wife of scientist André Delambre, Helene Delambre watches in horror as his teleportation experiments go awry, leaving him with the head and leg of a common housefly. Her devotion to her husband is demonstrated by her willingness to crush his hideous fly-head in a hydraulic press rather than see him continue to live a half-human, half-insect existence.

QUOTE: *"Oh André, I get so scared sometimes. The suddenness of our age! Electronics, rockets, Earth satellites, supersonic flight, and now this!"*

Inara

ORIGIN: Planet Sihnon
SOURCE: *Firefly* (TV series, 2002)

High-class courtesan Inara Serra books passage with Captain Mal Reynolds and the transport ship *Serenity* on TV's *Firefly*. An exotic beauty and practicing Buddhist, Inara sets aside her nonviolent beliefs when necessary, proving adept at martial arts, swordplay, and archery.

QUOTE: *"Would you like to lecture me the wickedness of my ways?"*

Iris

ORIGIN: 20th-century Earth
SOURCE: *The Angry Red Planet* (1960)

Amnesiac exobiologist Iris Ryan is one of only two survivors of an ill-fated mission to Mars in 1960's *The Angry Red Planet*. Her hypnosis-induced recollections of the expedition include encounters with several surreal Martian creatures—such as an intelligent amoeba—and much panicked screaming.

QUOTE: *"I know this is funny for a scientist, but maybe there are some things better left unknown."*

Jadzia

ORIGIN: Planet Trill
SOURCE: *Star Trek: Deep Space Nine* (TV series, 1993–1999)

Jadzia Dax is the Trill science officer aboard space station Deep Space Nine on TV's *Star Trek: Deep Space Nine*. The eighth Trill host of the symbiont Dax, Jadzia Dax is haunted by the legacy of its previous host, Curzon Dax. Mischievous in her youth, she eventually applies herself to her studies and earns degrees in exobiology, zoology, astrophysics, and exoarchaeology.

QUOTE: *"I think an honorable* victory *is better than an honorable defeat."*

Jaime

ORIGIN: 20th-century Earth
SOURCE: *The Bionic Woman* (TV series, 1976–1978)

Tennis pro Jaime Sommers overcomes the grievous injuries she suffers in a skydiving accident with the help of bionic enhancements devised by the Office of Scientific Information. As the world's first

"Bionic Woman," she is both a pioneer and an indispensable complement to her bionic soul mate Steve Austin.

TRIVIA: *Name of Jaime's "Bionic Dog": Maximillion.*

Janice

ORIGIN: 23rd-century Earth
SOURCE: *Star Trek* (TV series, 1966–1969)

Captain's yeoman Janice Rand proves a loyal and dedicated helpmate for Captain James T. Kirk of the USS *Enterprise*. The first in a long line of comely blonde yeomen, each outfitted in the same low-cut version of the regulation Starfleet uniform, Rand excels at her primary task of bringing her commanding officer a tray of food—an important step, apparently, on the road to her eventual promotion to transporter chief.

QUOTE: *"Captain, look at my legs!"*

Jessica

ORIGIN: 23rd-century Earth
SOURCE: *Logan's Run* (1976)

In the overpopulated future Earth depicted in the novel, film, and TV series *Logan's Run*, Jessica is a mysterious, alluring young woman who joins Logan in his race to escape the authorities who want to euthanize him in the name of population control.

QUOTE: *"We've been outside! There's another world outside!"*

Jillian

ORIGIN: 20th-century Earth
SOURCE: *Close Encounters of the Third Kind* (1977)

Muncie, Indiana, single mom Jillian Guiler has a "close encounter" with extraterrestrial visitors who probe her home and abduct her young son. Like Roy Neary—whom she later befriends—she is among the many humans drawn inexorably to Devil's Tower National Monument in Wyoming for a nighttime rendezvous with the alien "mothership."

QUOTE: *"I don't believe it's real. I don't believe it's real."*

Joanna

ORIGIN: 20th-century Earth
SOURCE: *The Stepford Wives* (1975)

Suburban housewives roll out the welcome wagon for their new neighbor Joanna Eberhart in 1975's *The Stepford Wives*, but she's a little creeped out by their automaton-like efficiency. She's on to something—they've been replaced by robots.

QUOTE: *"If I am wrong, I'm insane . . . but if I'm right, it's even worse than if I was wrong."*

JOYCE

ORIGIN: 20th-century Earth
SOURCE: *War of the Colossal Beast* (1958)

Joyce Manning is the concerned sister of "amazing colossal man" Glenn Manning in the 1958 B-movie *War of the Colossal Beast*. More assertive and less panicky than the typical 1950s B-movie heroine, Joyce Manning bravely takes charge after her hideously disfigured fifty-foot-tall radioactive mutant sibling is discovered alive and wreaking havoc in Mexico.

QUOTE: *"His face . . . I can't forget how horrible it was."*

JUBILATION

ORIGIN: 20th-century Earth
SOURCE: *Uncanny X-Men* #244 (Marvel Comics, 1989)

Jubilation Lee is the distinctive and apt name of the vivacious Chinese-American gymnast whose mutant ability to project energy bursts from her fingertips earns her a place among the X-Men as Jubilee. Orphaned in childhood, Jubilation has a rebellious streak and an infectious, spunky personality.

QUOTE: *"I don't have a clue about how to talk to normal kids my age."*

JUDY

ORIGIN: Future Earth
SOURCE: *The Jetsons* (TV series, 1962–1963)

With her love of fad dances and teen idols and her mortification at everything her parents say and do, George and Jane Jetson's beloved daughter, Judy, brings the vivacious energy of a mid-twentieth-century teenage bobby-soxer to Earth's utopian future on *The Jetsons*.

QUOTE: *"Daddy, if you dance like that in front of my friends I have to go live in another galaxy."*

JULIA

ORIGIN: 20th-century Oceania
SOURCE: *1984* by George Orwell (published 1949)

This attractive Ministry of Truth employee in the nightmarish police state of Oceania embarks upon a sexual relationship with her colleague Winston Smith in George Orwell's *1984*. A sensualist, Julia prefers to live in the moment rather than build the resistance movement with the committed Winston.

QUOTE: *"It's the one thing they can't do. They can make you say anything—anything—but they can't make you believe it."*

KATHRYN

ORIGIN: 24th-century Earth
SOURCE: *Star Trek: Voyager* (TV series, 1995–2001)

Variant form of Katherine used by Captain Kathryn Janeway, commander of a starship stranded in the far-flung Delta Quadrant on TV's *Star Trek: Voyager*. Strong-willed, demanding, and occasionally unconventional in her command decisions, this Kathryn does not seek love from her subordinates—only obedience and grudging respect.

QUOTE: *"One of the nice things about being captain is that you can keep some things to yourself."*

KATSURA

ORIGIN: 20th-century Earth
SOURCE: *Terror of Mechagodzilla* (1975)

Katsura is the name of a lovely deciduous tree native to Japan—and of the lovely cyborg daughter of a mad Japanese scientist in 1975's *Terror of Mechagodzilla*. Rebuilt with bionic parts following a laboratory accident, the shy, demure Katsura is used by evil aliens in a plot to unleash the mechanical monster known as Mechagodzilla on defenseless Japan.

QUOTE: *"I may look like a girl but I'm not. I'm a cyborg!"*

KAYLEE

ORIGIN: Unknown
SOURCE: *Firefly* (TV series, 2002)

Kaywinnit Lee "Kaylee" Frye is the vivacious ship's mechanic aboard the transport ship *Serenity* on TV's *Firefly*. Eternally upbeat, Kaylee is known as much for her sunny disposition as for her handiness with a wrench. She has a pronounced weakness for strawberries.

QUOTE: *"Hamsters is nice."*

KEiKO

ORIGIN: 24th-century Earth

SOURCE: *Star Trek: The Next Generation* (TV series, 1987–1994)

This lovely girl's name means "respectful child" in Japanese. Choose it for its beauty and to honor Keiko Ishikawa O'Brien, botanist, schoolteacher, and wife of transporter chief Miles O'Brien on *Star Trek: The Next Generation* and *Star Trek: Deep Space Nine*.

QUOTE: *"I am a teacher. My responsibility is to expose my students to knowledge, not hide it from them."*

Kristine

ORIGIN: 23rd-century Earth

SOURCE: *Red Dwarf* (BBC TV series, 1988–1999)

Variant form of Christine used by Kristine Kochanski, navigation officer aboard the mining vessel *Red Dwarf* on the eponymous BBC sci-fi comedy. She is the ex-girlfriend (and, due to a time anomaly, the mother) of third technician Dave Lister.

QUOTE: *"How did I end up like this? On a ship where the fourth most popular pastime is going down to the laundry room and watching my knickers spin dry?"*

Lana

ORIGIN: 20th-century Earth

SOURCE: *Superboy* #10 (DC Comics, 1950)

Lana Lang, the flame-haired, free-spirited Superman love interest and childhood friend of Clark Kent, is eventually supplanted by the more demure, less interesting Lois Lane. Lana's ardor for the Man of Steel often goes unrequited.

TRIVIA: *Lana Lang is one of many Superman characters with the initials "L. L." (see also Lara, below; Lex, p. 109; Linda, p. 21; and Lois, p. 87).*

Lara

ORIGIN: Planet Krypton

SOURCE: *Superman* comic strip (1939)

Loving wife of doomed Kryptonian scientist Jor-El and birth mother of Kal-El, the Kryptonian foundling who will later assume the Earth identity of Clark Kent/Superman. Though she could take the trip with him, Lara elects to stay and perish on Krypton to give baby Kal-El a better chance of making it to Earth safely in Jor-El's homemade rocket ship.

TRIVIA: *Lara's maiden name is Lara Lor-Van.*

Leia

ORIGIN: Planet Alderaan
SOURCE: *Star Wars* (1977)

The daughter of Anakin Skywalker, Leia Organa is adopted as a baby by the Royal Family of Alderaan. She grows up to become a surprisingly driven and dedicated princess—and the youngest member ever to serve in the Imperial Senate.

QUOTE: *"I don't know who you are or where you've come from, but from now on you'll do as I say, okay?"*

VARIANTS: *Lea, Leah, and Lia*

Lenina

ORIGIN: 26th-century Earth
SOURCE: *Brave New World* by Aldous Huxley (published 1932)

Often described as "pneumatic" (a futuristic euphemism for "buxom"), Lenina Crowne is one of the most desirable women on the utopian future Earth depicted in Aldous Huxley's *Brave New World*. A lab tech in the Central London Hatchery and Conditioning Centre, the promiscuous Lenina happily plays her assigned role in a society where sex and drugs serve to anesthetize the complacent, conformist population.

TRIVIA: *Huxley named the character of Lenina after the Soviet leader Vladimir Lenin.*

Lila

ORIGIN: 20th-century Earth
SOURCE: *The Thing with Two Heads* (1972; directed by Lee Frost)

Devoted ex-girlfriend of Jack Moss, a hulking, black death row inmate who has a white racist's head transplanted onto his body in the 1972 sci-fi shocker *The Thing with Two Heads*. Though she still carries a torch for Jack, Lila is somewhat put off by the presence of a raging cracker just over his left shoulder.

QUOTE: *"Do you have two of anything else?"*

LOiS

ORIGIN: 20th-century Earth

SOURCE: *Action Comics* #1 (1938)

Raven-haired newspaper reporter Lois Lane of Metropolis's *Daily Planet* becomes romantically involved (and later marries) the diffident lummox Clark Kent, alias Superman. Assertive, willful, and thorough, Lois has all the attributes of a great journalist.

TRIVIA: *Lois Lane's middle name is Joanne.*

LOri

ORIGIN: 21st-century Earth

SOURCE: *Total Recall* (1990)

Do not expect constancy from a daughter named after this faithless wife of Douglas Quaid in the 1990 film *Total Recall*. While Lori Quaid appears to be a devoted and loving spouse, she is actually merely posing as Quaid's wife at the behest of her sinister boyfriend, Richter.

QUOTE: *"Doug. Honey . . . you wouldn't hurt me, would you, sweetheart? Sweetheart, be reasonable. After all, we're married!"*

Lorraine

ORIGIN: 20th-century Earth

SOURCE: *Back to the Future* (1985)

Spunky 1950s teenager who develops a crush on *Back to the Future* time-traveler Marty McFly—never knowing that she is in fact his mother. A social butterfly with a rebellious streak, the pretty and popular Lorraine must ultimately be reconnected with her own future husband, George, in order to ensure Marty's existence and her own happiness in an altered timeline.

QUOTE: *"Marty, don't be such a square!"*

Luna

ORIGIN: 22nd-century Earth

SOURCE: *Sleeper* (1973)

Last name: Schlosser. Upper-middle-class poetess who befriends the cryogenically unfrozen health food store owner Miles Monroe in the year 2173 in Woody Allen's sci-fi comedy *Sleeper*. An amateur philosopher and patron of radical causes, Luna helps hook Miles up with the rebel underground looking to kidnap and assassinate the supreme leader's nose before it can be cloned.

QUOTE: *"Do you know that* God *spelled backwards is* dog?"

madeline

ORIGIN: 20th-century Earth
SOURCE: *Electric Dreams* (1984)

When cellist Madeline Robistat moves into the apartment upstairs from nebbishy architect Miles Harding, she not only beguiles him, but his newly self-aware computer Edgar too! Eighties icon Virginia Madsen plays the object of many a young computer geek's affections in the 1984 sci-fi romantic comedy *Electric Dreams*.

QUOTE: *"I like the way you look at the world . . . the way you make me smile."*

margaret

ORIGIN: 20th-century Earth
SOURCE: *Liquid Sky* (1982)

Gay, lesbian, and transgendered parents may want to opt for this once-popular, now old-fashioned girl's name used by the bisexual protagonist of 1982's *Liquid Sky*, about a woman whose lower Manhattan apartment building becomes a launching pad for alien invaders who feed off human endorphins.

QUOTE: *"Whether or not I like someone doesn't depend on what kind of genitals they have."*

marge

ORIGIN: 20th-century Earth
SOURCE: *I Married a Monster from Outer Space* (1958)

Bart Simpson's mom isn't the only fictional Marge with a less-than-ideal marriage. Contented 1950s homemaker Marge Bradley Farrell begins to freak out when her beloved husband, Bill, turns out to have a malevolent space alien inhabiting his body in the 1958 B-movie *I Married a Monster from Outer Space*.

QUOTE: *"I know you're not Bill, you're some thing that crept into Bill's body."*

VARIANTS: *Margie*

maria

ORIGIN: Future Earth

SOURCE: *Metropolis* (1927)

The ravishing leader of a group of subterranean worker drones in Fritz Lang's silent sci-fi masterpiece *Metropolis*, Maria leads a revolt against their pampered "thinker" overlords—but is ultimately replaced by a lookalike robot (the first such creation to appear in a film).

QUOTE: *"There can be no understanding between the hand and the brain unless the heart acts as mediator."*

marilyn

ORIGIN: 20th-century Earth

SOURCE: *Empire of the Ants* (1977)

Beautiful, unscrupulous realtor Marilyn Fryser peddles worthless plots of Florida swampland to unsuspecting rubes in 1977's *Empire of the Ants*. What she doesn't know, but will soon realize, is that the land is also home to hundreds of giant, mutated, carnivorous ants who summarily ingest her clientele.

TRIVIA: *Joan Collins reportedly called playing Marilyn Fryser the worst experience of her acting career.*

maureen

ORIGIN: 20th-century Earth

SOURCE: *Lost in Space* (TV series, 1965–1968)

Say "Here's to you, Mrs. Robinson" by naming your daughter after the able family matriarch played by June Lockhart on the popular 1960s TV series *Lost in Space*. The happiest of homemakers, even when stranded thousands of light years from Earth, Maureen Robinson excels at all the domestic arts, including baking, cooking, darning socks, making clothes, and doing the laundry.

QUOTE: *"We have no business trying to land on that planet. We're settlers, not explorers."*

may

ORIGIN: 20th-century Earth

SOURCE: *Amazing Fantasy* #15 (Marvel Comics, 1962)

This pleasant, once-fashionable girl's name perfectly suits Peter Parker's kindly, widowed Aunt May—an everlasting source of homemade soups and caring reminders to bundle up or take a sweater. Blissfully unaware of her nephew's secret identity as Spider-Man, May Parker nevertheless finds herself repeatedly threatened by his superpowered nemeses—at one point even marrying Dr. Octopus.

QUOTE: *"Oh, Peter, I'm so proud of you!"*

maya

ORIGIN: Planet Psychon
SOURCE: *Space: 1999* (TV series, 1975–1977)

This lovely girl's name, which in Hindu honors the divine creative force and in Nepali means "love," is apparently quite popular on the planet Psychon. The exotic-looking, mysterious Psychon metamorph Maya uses her shape-shifting abilities to save the crew of Moonbase Alpha from aliens on numerous occasions.

QUOTE: *"Is there some flaw in the Psychon nature that turns us all into monsters?"*

megan

ORIGIN: 20th-century Earth
SOURCE: *Mosquito* (1995)

Fresh-on-the-job park ranger who discovers a nest of giant mutant mosquitoes that have been transformed by the blood of space aliens who crash-landed in a U.S. National Park in the 1995 low-budget feature *Mosquito*.

QUOTE: *"I don't think this is a bird, Ray. It looks more like . . . some kind of bug!"*

mindy

ORIGIN: 20th-century Earth
SOURCE: *Mork and Mindy* (TV series, 1978–1982)

Winsome, plucky Mindy McConnell plays Desi to Robin Williams's antic Lucy, Mork from Ork, on the late 1970s sci-fi sitcom *Mork and Mindy*. Her kindness in helping the Orkan visitor adjust to life on Earth eventually blossoms into romance. The couple produce one child—though the means by which this interspecies spawning is achieved are never fully illuminated.

QUOTE: *"Mork, I have something to confess to you. When you were out one day, I . . . I . . . I put on your spacesuit."*

MOLLY

ORIGIN: Future Earth
SOURCE: "Johnny Mnemonic" by William Gibson (published 1981)

Molly Millions is the name of the cyborg "razor girl," armed to the teeth with cybernetic enhancements, who appears in several novels and stories by the cyberpunk pioneer William Gibson. A ruthless mercenary, she has also used the aliases Sally Shears and Rose Kolodny.

QUOTE: *"Name's Millions. Molly Millions. You want to get out of here, boss? People are starting to stare."*

montana

ORIGIN: 20th-century Earth
SOURCE: *Slaughterhouse-Five* by Kurt Vonnegut (published 1953)

Nubile young actress and model Montana Wildhack is kidnapped by aliens from the planet Tralfamadore and forced to mate with time-tripping optometrist Billy Pilgrim in a geodesic zoo in Kurt Vonnegut's novel *Slaughterhouse-Five*.

QUOTE: *"You don't meet many gentlemen in the entertainment industry."*

NANCY

ORIGIN: 20th-century Earth
SOURCE: *Attack of the 50-Foot Woman* (1958)

Your daughter won't be anybody's pushover if you go with this old-fashioned girl's name. In 1958's *Attack of the 50-Foot Woman*, mousey housewife Nancy Archer suffers innumerable domestic indignities at the hands of her cheating husband and domineering father. But she turns the tables after an alien spacecraft zaps her with a ray that turns her into a butt-kicking giantess.

QUOTE: *"I know where my husband is! He's with that woman!"*

nanelia

ORIGIN: Deep space
SOURCE: *Battle Beyond the Stars* (1980)

This Hebrew name meaning "grace" may have fallen out of favor on Earth, but it survives in the deep-space milieu of 1980's *Battle Beyond the Stars*, where it's used by the comely daughter of Dr. Hephaestus. Raised by her father on a space station with only her singing androids for company, Nanelia falls hard for the winsome Akira visitor Shad.

TRIVIA: *Nanelia's studies onboard her father's science station appear to include the comparative mating practices of various alien species.*

nell

ORIGIN: Unknown
SOURCE: *Battle Beyond the Stars* (1980)
Opinionated talking spaceship Nell ferries the young Akir native Shad on his mission to recruit mercenaries to help liberate his planet from the evil Sador in the 1980 B-movie space opera *Battle Beyond the Stars*. Her "personality" appears to be that of a vain, hectoring, middle-aged woman.

QUOTE: *"If they ever start giving out prizes for running away, you'll be champion of the universe!"*

niki

ORIGIN: 20th-century Earth
SOURCE: *Spacehunter: Adventures in the Forbidden Zone* (1983)
Spunky teenage pixie (played by Molly Ringwald) who accompanies the jaded space adventurer Wolff on his journey to the fortress of Overdog to rescue three Earth women in the 1983 space opera *Spacehunter: Adventures in the Forbidden Zone*. Equal parts con artist and junior-grade Sacagawea, Niki wins Wolff's trust with her skills as a guide, though her personal hygiene fails to impress.

QUOTE: *"What do you think I am, you scrawny earthbag? I'm a woman!"*

nova

ORIGIN: Post-apocalyptic Earth
SOURCE: *Planet of the Apes* (1968)
Mute human female, usually attired in tattered rags that show off her ample curves, who becomes first the cellmate and later the concubine of Taylor, the twentieth-century astronaut stranded on a post-apocalyptic Earth ruled by simians in *Planet of the Apes*. Possessed of an earthy sensuality but little or no intellect, Nova

somehow manages to overcome her linguistic limitations to scream out one line of dialogue over the course of two movies.

QUOTE: *"Taylor!"*

nyota

ORIGIN: 23rd-century Earth

SOURCE: *Star Trek* (TV series, 1966–1969)

This lovely African name means "star" in Swahili and pays homage to the chief communications officer of the USS *Enterprise*, the beautiful and resourceful Nyota Uhura. A child given this name may be ticketed for a musical career. Uhura sings and accompanies herself on the Vulcan harp on numerous occasions.

QUOTE: *"Sometimes I think if I hear that word* frequency *one more time, I'll cry."*

ororo

ORIGIN: 20th-century Earth

SOURCE: *Giant Size X-Men* #1 (Marvel Comics, 1975)

Ororo Munroe is the birth name of Storm, one of the most popular and powerful members of the X-Men. The daughter of a Kenyan princess and an African-American photojournalist, this ravishing blue-eyed, white-haired mutant possesses nearly unlimited dominion over the weather. Confident and courageous, she grows over time into one of the acknowledged leaders of the team.

QUOTE: *"Do you know what happens to a toad when it's struck by lightning? The same thing that happens to everything else."*

paula

ORIGIN: 20th-century Earth

SOURCE: *Plan 9 from Outer Space* (1959)

Devoted wife of Jeff Trent, the airline pilot hero of the low-budget 1959 feature *Plan 9 from Outer Space*. Though a bit obtuse, Paula fulfills her principal function of screaming and being chased by zombies with admirable aplomb.

QUOTE: *"A flying saucer? You mean the kind from up there?"*

penny

ORIGIN: 20th-century Earth

SOURCE: *Lost in Space* (TV series, 1965–1968)

Penny Roberta Robinson is the youngest daughter of stranded space settlers John and Maureen Robinson in the popular 1960s TV series *Lost in Space*. Outgoing and intelligent, this tomboyish 12-year-old has an active imagination that occasionally gets her into dangerous situations.

TRIVIA: *Before leaving Earth for Alpha Centauri, Penny was elected president of her hometown chapter of the Space Scouts, an organization devoted to training the planetary colonizers of tomorrow.*

RACHAEL

ORIGIN: 21st-century Earth
SOURCE: *Blade Runner* (1982)

Variant form of Rachel used by the alluring female replicant who beguiles jaded "blade runner" Rick Deckard in a future Los Angeles, where the artificial life forms are hunted down and terminated.

QUOTE: *"Are these questions testing whether I'm a replicant or a lesbian, Mr. Deckard?"*

RAVEN

ORIGIN: 20th-century Earth
SOURCE: *Ms. Marvel* #17 (Marvel Comics, 1978)

Mysterious, exotic Raven Darkholme joins the X-Men after a tour of duty on the dark side with the Brotherhood of Evil Mutants. Better known as Mystique, the enigmatic mutant—who may be as old as 100—possesses the ability to change her cellular structure at will.

TRIVIA: *Mystique's many aliases include Leni Zauber, Amichai Benvenisti, and Mallory Brickman.*

RIVER

ORIGIN: Planet Osiris
SOURCE: *Firefly* (TV series, 2002)

Precocious but troubled teen River Tam stows away aboard *Serenity*, the ship transporting her brother Simon on TV's *Firefly*. Intellectually gifted and possessed of quasi-telepathic powers, River is nonetheless emotionally and psychologically unstable, a consequence of government-run brain experiments. She is prone to making oracular, syntactically tortuous pronouncements.

QUOTE: *"I get confused. I remember everything. I remember too much. And . . . some of it's made up, and . . . some of it can't be quantified, and . . . there's secrets . . . and . . ."*

ROSIE

ORIGIN: Future Earth

SOURCE: *The Jetsons* (TV series, 1962–1963)

Robot maid employed by the futuristic Jetson family on the eponymous cartoon series. Renowned for her pineapple upside-down cake, the tart-tongued yet sensitive Rosie may be named after World War II factory icon Rosie the Riveter.

QUOTE: *"I swear on my mother's rechargeable batteries."*

VARIANTS: *Rose, Roseann*

SALLY

ORIGIN: 20th-century Earth

SOURCE: *The Brain from Planet Arous* (1957)

This retro girl's name may be due for a comeback. If it suggests a sweet, supportive 1950s-era female, you may be thinking of Charlie Brown's sister or Sally Fallon, the devoted fiancée of a scientist possessed by a criminal alien brain in the 1957 B-movie *The Brain from Planet Arous*.

QUOTE: *"You know it's three o'clock and you mad scientists haven't even stopped for lunch?"*

SANDRA

ORIGIN: 20th-century Earth

SOURCE: *The Bees* (1978)

United Nations bee researcher Sandra Miller tries desperately to convince the world body to reason with a swarm of sentient killer bees bent on stopping mankind from polluting the environment in the alarmist 1978 insect invasion feature *The Bees*.

QUOTE: *"You have to listen! You have to listen to what the bees have to say!"*

SARAH JANE

ORIGIN: 20th-century Earth

SOURCE: *Dr. Who* (BBC TV series, 1963–present)

Investigative journalist Sarah Jane Smith accompanies the Time Lord known as the Doctor on his travels through time and space during his third and fourth regenerations. Plucky and opinionated, Sarah Jane chafes against the chauvinistic attitudes and professional limitations imposed on women by men.

QUOTE: *"This isn't South Croydon!"*

sonia

ORIGIN: 20th-century Earth

SOURCE: *Abraxas, Guardian of the Universe* (1991)

If you foresee an important maternal role for your unborn daughter—particularly one with galactic implications—why not name her after this character from *Abraxas, Guardian of the Universe*? Sonia Murray is an ordinary Earth woman who carries a child with the secret to the all-important "anti-life equation."

QUOTE: *"Think you space guys or whatever it is you are could have dropped me a note or something? You know, just to let me know that I'm not crazy?"*

Stella

ORIGIN: Unknown

SOURCE: *Starcrash* (1979)

When the creators of *Starcrash* crafted their 1979 Italian-made *Star Wars* knockoff, they helpfully reimagined Han Solo as a bodacious female. Stella Star is the best spaceship pilot in the galaxy, as easy on the eyes as she is effortless in her kung-fu moves. You won't be raising a wallflower if you name your daughter after this audacious rocket jockey.

QUOTE: *"Go for hyperspace!"*

sylvia

ORIGIN: 20th-century Earth

SOURCE: *The War of the Worlds* (1953)

Last name: Van Buren. Fetching young daughter of a small-town pastor who falls in love with stolid scientist Clayton Forrester in the 1953 film adaptation of H. G. Wells's *War of the Worlds*.

QUOTE: *"They murder everything that moves."*

Talia

ORIGIN: 23rd-century Earth

SOURCE: *Babylon 5* (TV series, 1994–1998)

A member of Psi Corps, Talia Winters is assigned to Babylon 5 as a "commercial telepath," putting her telepathic powers to work brokering business deals on the space station. A trusted aide to the station's commanders—and the object of security chief Michael Garibaldi's affections—Talia must return to Earth after a hidden "sleeper personality" controlled by Psi Corps takes over her body.

QUOTE: *"The corps is mother! The corps is father! You're dead, Lyta Alexander! We'll find you! The corps will find you!"*

TaLLeaH

ORIGIN: Planet Venus
SOURCE: *Queen of Outer Space* (1958)

Venusian scientist (with an unexplained Hungarian accent) who plots to overthrow her planet's evil queen in the 1958 B-movie *Queen of Outer Space.*

QUOTE: *"If love is what makes your heart tick, then I love you too."*

Tanna

ORIGIN: Unknown
SOURCE: *Plan 9 from Outer Space* (1959)

Alien who assists Eros in his scheme to conquer the Earth with a zombie army in the low-budget 1959 feature *Plan 9 from Outer Space.* Tanna does not fully share her superior's disdain for humanity and repeatedly questions his decisions.

QUOTE: *"Eros, do we* have *to kill them?"*

TaSHa

ORIGIN: 24th-century Earth
SOURCE: *Star Trek: The Next Generation* (TV series, 1987–1994)

The short form of Natasha (the Russian form of Natalie) and the name of the first, doomed security officer of the USS *Enterprise* under Captain Jean-Luc Picard. Killed by a malevolent oil slick in the episode "Skin of Evil," Tasha redeems her "empty death" by volunteering to die again in an alternate timeline. Instead she is captured and delivered into sexual slavery by the Romulans.

QUOTE: *"I've always known the risks that came with a Starfleet uniform. If I'm to die in one, I'd like my death to count for something."*

TeGan

ORIGIN: 20th-century Earth
SOURCE: *Dr. Who* (BBC TV series, 1963–present)

Australian flight attendant who brings a tart tongue and a penchant for tight-fitting leather miniskirts to *Dr. Who* as a trusted companion of the Time Lord known as the Doctor during his fourth and fifth regenerations. An outspoken Brisbane native who eventually flees the TARDIS after a violent encounter with the Daleks, Tegan often bickers with the Doctor and her fellow companions.

QUOTE: *"I'm just a head on legs!"*

TEYLA

ORIGIN: Planet Athos
SOURCE: *Stargate Atlantis* (TV series, 2004–present)

Teyla Emmagan is the beautiful native of a decimated alien world who joins forces with the *Stargate Atlantis* team in their efforts to defeat the hive-based parasitic species known as the Wraith. The ultimate survivor, Teyla ably serves the team with both her martial arts skills and her vast knowledge about the people and worlds Atlantis encounters.

QUOTE: *"Atlantis is far more than shelter, it is* hope. *Not only for our people but for everyone who would stand against the Wraith."*

T'PRING

ORIGIN: Planet Vulcan
SOURCE: *Star Trek* (TV series, 1966–1969)

Ravishing Vulcan beauty, betrothed in childhood to the USS *Enterprise*'s Mr. Spock but utterly disinterested in marrying him. Put off by the demands of a long-distance relationship, the eminently logical T'Pring connives to have Spock killed during their wedding ceremony so that she can marry his stolid, stay-at-home rival Stonn.

QUOTE: *"Spock. Parted from me and never parted. Never and always touching and touched. I await you."*

TRILLIAN

ORIGIN: 20th-century Earth
SOURCE: *The Hitchhiker's Guide to the Galaxy* (BBC Radio, 1978)

Name adopted by Tricia McMillan, a nubile astrophysicist from Earth who accompanies Zaphod Beebelbrox on his intergalactic journey aboard the starship *Heart of Gold* in Douglas Adams's *The Hitchhiker's Guide to the Galaxy*.

TRIVIA: *The Trillian instant messaging application was named after this character.*

Valerie

ORIGIN: 20th-century Earth
SOURCE: *Earth Girls Are Easy* (1989)

Gangly female manicurist who hooks up with a gangly male space alien on the rebound from a bad relationship in the 1989 sci-fi comedy *Earth Girls Are Easy*. Unlucky at love, the sweet-natured salon employee agrees to do a makeover on her extraterrestrial visitor after he and his spaceship comrades crash land in her swimming pool. Romance ensues.

QUOTE: *"I'm from the Valley. You're an alien. We might not even be anatomically compatible."*

Veronica

ORIGIN: 20th-century Earth
SOURCE: *The Fly* (1986)

Inquisitive journalist Veronica Quaife gets a little too close to her subject—eccentric scientist turned household pest Seth Brundle—in the 1986 version of *The Fly*. Fascinated at first with his teleportation experiments, and then with Brundle himself, she must ultimately kill the man she loves to prevent the revolting "Brundlefly" from completely subsuming his humanity.

QUOTE: *"Be afraid. Be very afraid."*

Vickie

ORIGIN: United Robotronics laboratory, 20th-century Earth
SOURCE: *Small Wonder* (TV series, 1985–1989)

Adorable little girl robot from the popular syndicated television sitcom of the late 1980s. The titular marvel is the handiwork of robotics engineer Ted Lawson, who brings her home to his family to be passed off as his adopted daughter. However, Vickie's super strength and speed, along with the presence of several unsightly electrical inputs on her body, raises the suspicion of the Lawsons' buttinsky neighbors, Brandon and Bonnie Brindle, and their inquisitive daughter, Harriet.

TRIVIA: *The name Vickie derives from the robot child's model name: Voice Input Child Identicant (V.I.C.I.)*

VARIANTS: *Victoria, Vicki*

WILMA

ORIGIN: 20th-century Earth
SOURCE: *Buck Rogers* comic strip (1929)

As resourceful as she is ravishing, Wilma Deering accompanies her lover Buck Rogers on his journeys through space in the twenty-fifth century. Often seen assisting resident "science guy" Dr. Huer, she has an adventurous streak of her own which often ends up getting her caught up in dangerous situations.

TRIVIA: *Invariably depicted as a blonde, Wilma was played as a brunette by Erin Gray in the revisionist 1979 TV series* Buck Rogers in the 25th Century.

ZARABETH

ORIGIN: Planet Sarpeidon
SOURCE: *Star Trek* (TV series, 1966–1969)

This distinctive girl's name, combining Zara (a form of Sarah) and Beth, is apparently quite popular on the doomed planet Sarpeidon in the twenty-third century. Sarpeidonite beauty Zarabeth is exiled into the planet's ice age via the atavachron time portal in the *Star Trek* episode "All Our Yesterdays."

QUOTE: *"Do you know what it's like alone, really alone? To send me here alone—if that is not death, what is?"*

ZOE

ORIGIN: 21st-century Earth
SOURCE: *Dr. Who* (BBC TV series, 1963–present)

This Greek name meaning "life" honors Zoe Heriot, a brilliant twenty-first-century astrophysicist who accompanies the second incarnation of the Time Lord known as the Doctor on his travels through time and space.

QUOTE: *"It's rude to point, you know. Especially with a gun."*

OTHER NOTABLE SCI-FI ZOES: *Zoë Washburne (Mal's loyal second-in-command,* Firefly*).*

CHAPTER 4

POWER NAMES

An aptly bestowed name can point a child in the direction you want him or her to go. Name a child Jeeves, as the comedian Jerry Seinfeld once pointed out, and the chances are good he will end up a butler. So if your designs for your offspring include supervillainy, planetary dominion, or garden-variety malevolence, select one of these powerful monikers drawn from the ranks of sci-fi baddies, monarchs, and warriors. Rest assured, your kid will never be messed with on the playground.

ALDO

ORIGIN: 20th-century Earth
SOURCE: *Battle for the Planet of the Apes* (1973)

Thuggish gorilla general whose unwillingness to coexist peacefully with humans nearly sparks a simian civil war in *Battle for the Planet of the Apes*.

QUOTE: *"You will call me by my proper rank—general!"*

BORiS

ORIGIN: 20th-century Earth
SOURCE: *Tales of Suspense* #69 (Marvel Comics, 1965)

Also known as Bullski the Merciless, Commissar Boris Bullski is better known to comic book fans as the impregnable Iron Man villain Titanium Man. This former Soviet army officer, with his suit of green titanium armor built with Gulag labor, represents the pinnacle of Communist Russian technology in service of world domination.

TRIVIA: *With his fellow supervillain Magneto (see Erik, p. 105), Titanium Man is the subject of a song on ex-Beatle Paul McCartney's 1975 album* Venus and Mars.

BUBBa

ORIGIN: Future Earth
SOURCE: *Mad Max* (1979)

Taciturn motorcycle gang member Bubba Zanetti has little to say in the post-apocalyptic sci-fi action-adventure feature *Mad Max*, but with his black leather motorcycle jacket, silver helmet with reflective visor, and Broomhandle Mauser pistol, he is one of sci-fi cinema's most stylish villains.

QUOTE: *"Joviality is a game of children."*

caesar

ORIGIN: 20th-century Earth
SOURCE: *Conquest of the Planet of the Apes* (1972)

To raise a future leader of men, choose this name used by the charismatic leader of the ape rebellion coming in Earth's near future. This cunning chimpanzee son of Cornelius and Zira cannily conceals his intelligence from the human authorities, waiting for the right moment to spark the uprising of simian slaves that results in the overthrow of Earth's government.

QUOTE: *"Where there is fire, there is smoke. And in that smoke, from this day forward, my people will crouch and conspire and plot and plan for the inevitable day of man's downfall."*

CHRISTOF

ORIGIN: 20th-century Earth
SOURCE: *The Truman Show* (1998)

Amoral television impresario who creates and produces a long-running series in which an unwitting man's "life" is broadcast to millions worldwide in the 1998 feature *The Truman Show*. A Svengali-like figure who speaks in corporate babble and controls every aspect of Truman's world from his sky-high redoubt, Christof is one of 1990s sci-fi's creepiest, most oleaginous villains.

QUOTE: *"Cue the sun!"*

CLARENCE

ORIGIN: 21st-century Earth
SOURCE: *Robocop* (1987)

Last name: Boddicker. Gangland kingpin who terrorizes the city of Old Detroit in Earth's dystopian near future. A vicious killer, Boddicker meets a violent end when the crime-fighting cyborg known as Robocop stabs him through the carotid artery with his six-inch-long titanium spiked knuckle duster.

QUOTE: *"See, I got this problem. Cops don't like me. So I don't like cops."*

DAMON

ORIGIN: 21st-century Earth
SOURCE: *The Running Man* (1987)

On a totalitarian future Earth, Damon Killian is the host of *The Running Man*, a reality game show where condemned criminals run for their lives from chainsaw-wielding goons. Not so much evil as dangerously amoral, this Damon is consumed with maximizing his audience share, no matter what the human cost.

QUOTE: *"This is television. That's all it is. It has nothing to do with people. It's to do with ratings!"*

Darryl

ORIGIN: 20th-century Earth
SOURCE: *Scanners* (1981)

Darryl Revok is the ruthless leader of an army of renegade telepaths in the 1981 sci-fi shocker *Scanners*. Bent on achieving world domination through dictatorial control of all his fellow "scanners," Darryl instills fear in his troops by making people's heads explode.

QUOTE: *"We're gonna do this the scanner way. I'm gonna suck your brain dry!"*

Darth

ORIGIN: Unknown
SOURCE: *Star Wars* (1977)

In *Star Wars* mythology, "Darth" precedes the title of a Sith Lord. Darth Vader, the malevolent black-helmeted villain of *Star Wars: A New Hope* and ensuing films in the cycle, is probably the most famous Sith Lord to hold that title.

TRIVIA: *Though its origins are obscure, Darth may be a combination of the words "Dark" and "Death."*

Davros

ORIGIN: Planet Skaro
SOURCE: *Dr. Who* (BBC TV series, 1963–present)

Megalomaniacal madman, creator of the Daleks. A brilliant scientist of the Kaled race on the planet Skaro, scarred and crippled in childhood, now permanently confined to a mobile life support chair. Davros seeks celestial domination through his army of mutants in mechanized casings.

QUOTE: *"You cannot kill me! I am Davros!"*

Eldon

ORIGIN: 21st-century Earth
SOURCE: *Blade Runner* (1982)

The enigmatic head of the Tyrell Corporation, Dr. Eldon Tyrell is responsible for the creation of the highly sophisticated artificial life forms known as replicants. A genetic-engineering pioneer and ruthless corporate baron in a dystopian future Los Angeles, Tyrell is ultimately killed by one of his own creations.

QUOTE: *"'More human than human' is our motto."*

EMILIO

ORIGIN: 20th-century Earth
SOURCE: *The Adventures of Buckaroo Banzai Across the 8th Dimension* (1984)

The archenemy of Buckaroo Banzai, the antic, cackling Dr. Emilio Lizardo is a mad Italian physicist possessed by an evil alien from the eighth dimension named Lord John Whorfin.

QUOTE: *"Laugh while you can, monkey-boy."*

ERIK

ORIGIN: 20th-century Earth
SOURCE: *X-Men* #1 (Marvel Comics, 1963)

This variant form of Eric perfectly captures the monomaniacal designs of Erik Magnus Lehnsherr, the costumed comic book supervillain known as Magneto. A Holocaust survivor and old friend of X-Men founder Charles Xavier, Lehnsherr turns evil out of a misguided conviction that a genocidal conflict between mutants and normal humans is inevitable.

QUOTE: *"Even an everyman with a kind heart becomes a rabid beast at the sight of that which he does not understand."*

EROS

ORIGIN: Unknown
SOURCE: *Plan 9 from Outer Space* (1959)

Eros is the project manager of an alien plot to conquer the Earth using the resurrected corpses of recently buried humans in the low-budget 1959 feature *Plan 9 from Outer Space*. This imperious "grave robber from outer space" is distinguished by his low opinion of Earthlings, whose "stupid minds" he blames for the species' limited achievements.

QUOTE: *"All you of Earth are idiots!"*

FENDER

ORIGIN: Post-apocalyptic Earth
SOURCE: *Cyborg* (1989)

Nefarious villain Fender Tremolo (named for the vibrating "whammy" bar on a Fender electric guitar) terrorizes the plague-ravaged future Earth milieu of 1989's *Cyborg* with his marauding band of murderous hooligans.

QUOTE: *"I like the death! I like the misery! I like this world!"*

Galan

ORIGIN: Planet Taa
SOURCE: *Fantastic Four* #48 (Marvel Comics, 1966)

Real name of the gluttonous planet consumer known as Galactus. Once an ordinary space explorer from the doomed planet Taa, Galan is transformed into the fearsome Devourer of Worlds by the cosmic entity known as Eternity. Endowed with the awesome Power Cosmic, Galactus now roams sharklike through the universe, looking for unsuspecting planets on which to feed.

QUOTE: *"Though I ravage worlds to live, I bear no malice to any living thing. I simply do what I must to survive."*

Gar

ORIGIN: Unknown
SOURCE: *Star Crystal* (1986)

Slimy, spike-tentacled alien life form who sucks the blood out of helpless space shuttle crewmembers in the low-budget 1986 *Alien* knockoff *Star Crystal*. Though he at first appears to be a murderous beast, Gar has a conversion after reading the Bible on the shuttle's computer and reveals that he killed only in self-defense.

QUOTE: *"Through your computer I learned your lack of respect for life."*

Gor

ORIGIN: Planet Arous
SOURCE: *The Brain from Planet Arous* (1957)

Enormous floating alien brain who takes possession of scientist Steve March's body in the 1957 B-movie *The Brain from Planet Arous*. A sadistic criminal on the lam from the Arousian authorities, Gor is pleasantly surprised when his dormant libido is activated by March's girlfriend Sally.

QUOTE: *"I am Gor! I need your body as a dwelling-place while I am here on your planet Earth."*

Gort

ORIGIN: Unknown
SOURCE: *The Day the Earth Stood Still* (1951)

Hulking metallic robot who accompanies the galactic peace emissary Klaatu on his mission to Earth in the 1951 sci-fi classic *The Day the Earth Stood Still*. Though he at first functions as Klaatu's bodyguard, Gort eventually uses his awesome destructive power to deter Earth's bickering world leaders from settling their disputes through violence.

TRIVIA: *Gort is called Gnut in the short story on which* The Day the Earth Stood Still *is based.*

GRODD

ORIGIN: 20th-century Earth
SOURCE: *The Flash* #106 (DC Comics, 1959)

Superstrong, telepathic gorilla supervillain who typically matches wits with his archenemy the Flash in DC comic books. Endowed with super intelligence by a visiting space alien, this once quite typical jungle simian now uses his mind control powers in the service of a megalomaniacal war on humanity.

QUOTE: *"There's more than one way to peel a banana."*

HECTOR

ORIGIN: Unknown
SOURCE: *Saturn 3* (1980)

Menacing robot assistant used by the unhinged Captain Benson to terrorize the two-person crew of an outer-space food research station in the 1980 film *Saturn 3*. The prototype of the "Demigod" series, the enormous gleaming metallic golem eventually turns on its master after falling in lust with the object of his affections, a female research assistant played by Farrah Fawcett.

QUOTE: *"I am not malfunctioning—you are."*

HUMUNGUS

ORIGIN: Future Earth
SOURCE: *The Road Warrior* (1981)

The leader of a nomadic horde of murderous motorcycle punks, masked goon Lord Humungus finds himself drawn into mortal conflict with Mad Max when he besieges the wrong oil refinery in the 1981 sequel *The Road Warrior*.

QUOTE: *"Fear is our ally. The gasoline will be ours. Then you shall have your revenge!"*

Kang

ORIGIN: Planet Rigel 7

SOURCE: *The Simpsons* (TV series, 1990–)

Kang is the male half of the brother-and-sister team of drooling, one-eyed, octopus-like aliens from the planet Rigel 7 who occasionally menace the city of Springfield on the animated comedy series *The Simpsons*. His sister is Kodos.

QUOTE: *"We have reached the limits of what rectal probing can teach us."*

OTHER NOTABLE SCI-FI KANGS: *Kang (Klingon nemesis,* Star Trek*)*

Khan

ORIGIN: 20th-century Earth

SOURCE: *Star Trek* (TV series, 1966–1969)

Derived from an ancient Persian title meaning "commander," Khan is also the name of one of the most feared men in the universe: Khan Noonien Singh, the leader of a group of genetically engineered supermen in the *Star Trek* episode "Space Seed." Defrosted from a three-hundred-year cryogenic freeze by the starship *Enterprise* crew, Khan uses his superior will and guile to take over the ship. Virile and domineering, Khan firmly believes in his genetically predetermined right to rule other men—and to bring the women he desires to heel.

QUOTE: *"Improve a mechanical device and you may double productivity. But improve man, you gain a thousandfold."*

Kimar

ORIGIN: Planet Mars

SOURCE: *Santa Claus Conquers the Martians* (1964)

Martian council leader whose children's listlessness inspires the Red Planet's plan to abduct Santa Claus, the benevolent Earth gift-bringer, and deliver him to Mars to service its joyless population. At heart a concerned parent, Kimar finds his evil tempered and eventually overcome by his appreciation for the Christmas spirit.

QUOTE: *"Santa, you will never return to Earth. You belong to Mars now!"*

Kodos

ORIGIN: Planet Rigel 7

SOURCE: *The Simpsons* (TV series, 1990–)

Kodos is the female half of the brother-and-sister team of drooling, one-eyed, octopus-like aliens from the planet Rigel 7 who occasionally menace the citizens of Springfield on the animated comedy series *The Simpsons*. Her brother, Kang, played Bob Dole to Kodos's Bill Clinton in the extraterrestrial duo's attempt to hijack the 1996 presidential election.

QUOTE: *"It's true, we are aliens. But what are you going to do about it? It's a two-party system!"*

LEX
ORIGIN: 20th-century Earth
SOURCE: *Action Comics* #23 (1940)
Short form of Alexander preferred by Alexander Joseph Luthor, a megalomaniacal scientist who proves to be Superman's most dogged foe. An imposing physical specimen with bald head and maniacal mien, Lex Luthor possesses no superpowers of his own, relying instead on his scientific acumen, guile, and knack for acquiring and wielding power in his schemes to take control of the planet.

TRIVIA: *Luthor's hatred for Superman may stem in part from the hero's role in the chemical spill that caused his premature baldness.*

LOCUTUS
ORIGIN: Borg mothership
SOURCE: *Star Trek: The Next Generation* (TV series, 1987–1994)
This Latin term meaning "he who has spoken" is adopted by USS *Enterprise* captain Jean-Luc Picard after his assimilation by the marauding hive-minded alien race known as the Borg. As Locutus, Picard leads the Borg to victory at the Battle of Wolf 359, using knowledge absorbed from the starship commander's mind to outwit and annihilate the thirty-nine starships sent to repel the Borg invasion of Earth.

QUOTE: *"Resistance is futile."*

MATTHIAS
ORIGIN: Post-apocalyptic Earth
SOURCE: *The Omega Man* (1971)
One-time TV newscaster turned charismatic leader of "The

Family," a band of ravenous, roving vampire-zombies who torment the few remaining human survivors of a plague-ravaged Earth in the 1971 feature *The Omega Man*.

QUOTE: *"Definition of a scientist—a man who understands nothing until there is nothing left to understand."*

maximilian

ORIGIN: Unknown
SOURCE: *The Black Hole* (1979)

Fearsome scarlet robot who carries out the orders of the evil Dr. Hans Reinhardt in the 1979 film *The Black Hole*. He is outwitted and disabled by the tiny, feckless robot drone, V.I.N.CENT.

TRIVIA: *Contrary to popular belief, Maximilian was not named after Maximilian Schell, the actor who plays his master, Hans Reinhardt.*

maxwell

ORIGIN: 20th-century Earth
SOURCE: *Amazing Spider-Man* #9 (Marvel Comics, 1964)

Electric lineman Maxwell Dillon is transformed into the jumpsuit-clad master of electricity known as Electro after a freak lightning strike triggers a mutagenic change in his nervous system. Endowed with dominion over one of the world's most powerful forces, Maxwell sees his authoritarian tendencies (born of a deep-seated inferiority complex) come to the fore and lead him to a career in supervillainy.

QUOTE: *"Let's see you dodge this electric bolt, you overconfident braggart!"*

ming

ORIGIN: Planet Mongo
SOURCE: *Flash Gordon* comic strip (1934)

Tyrannical ruler of the planet Mongo, known to his oppressed subjects as Ming the Merciless. A vicious despot who uses death rays and killer robots to keep his people in line, Ming usurps the throne from its rightful occupant, Prince Barin. His only weakness is his love for Flash Gordon's curvaceous inamorata, Dale Arden.

QUOTE: *"Pathetic earthlings! Hurling your bodies out into the void, without the slightest inkling of who or what is out here."*

MUSTAPHA

ORIGIN: 26th-century Earth
SOURCE: *Brave New World* by Aldous Huxley (published 1932)

As Resident World Controller for Western Europe, Mustapha Mond (whose last name means "world" in French) is one of the most powerful officials of the utopian future depicted in Aldous Huxley's *Brave New World*. A former scientist, Mond now spends his time censoring other people's scientific discoveries and persecuting anyone whose unorthodox beliefs threaten the World State's concept of a stable society. He does, however, keep copies of several banned books in a safe in his office for his personal perusal.

QUOTE: *"God in the safe and Ford on the shelves."*

OMUS

ORIGIN: Delta 3
SOURCE: *The Shape of Things to Come* (1979)

Power-crazed tyrant from the planet Delta 3 who tries to blackmail Earth into submission in the 1979 *Star Wars* knockoff *The Shape of Things to Come*. For a supposed evil genius, he is defeated with surprising ease by a ragtag band of misfits and cute robots.

QUOTE: *"You are the one who inspired me, taught me to place science above all else!"*

OTTO

ORIGIN: 20th-century Earth
SOURCE: *Amazing Spider-Man* #3 (Marvel Comics, 1963)

Renowned nuclear physicist Dr. Otto Octavius joins the ranks of the world's most notorious supervillains after his atomic experiments drive him criminally insane. Endowed with the ability to control four mechanical "arms" with the power of thought alone, he christens himself Dr. Octopus and embarks on a life of megalomaniacal mayhem. His plans are invariably thwarted by his arch-nemesis, Spider-Man.

QUOTE: *"Between my own super-strength and the atomic power which is mine to command, I'm the strongest man alive!"*

PALPATINE

ORIGIN: Planet Naboo
SOURCE: *Star Wars: The Phantom Menace* (1999)

Also known as Darth Sidious, this ambitious, cunning Sith Lord hails from the Planet Naboo, where he was born into a noble family with the name Palpatine. His signature contribution to *Star Wars* mythology lies in manipulating Anakin Skywalker over to the Dark Side and a new identity as Darth Vader.

QUOTE: *"And you, young Skywalker; we shall watch your career with great interest."*

Quentin

ORIGIN: 20th-century Earth
SOURCE: *Amazing Spider-Man* #13 (Marvel Comics, 1964)

Former movie stuntman Quentin Beck channels frustration over his dead-end job in the film industry into a lucrative second career as the comic book supervillain Mysterio. Principally assigned to menace Spider-Man, Mysterio uses the power of illusion and his expertise in special effects to bedevil his opponents and accrue ill-gotten power.

QUOTE: *"You haven't won yet, Spider-Man!"*

Sador

ORIGIN: Planet Malmori
SOURCE: *Battle Beyond the Stars* (1980)

Only truly evil designs for your child would possess you to name your child after this villainous Malmori despot, who subjugates the peaceful people of Akir in the 1980 B-movie space opera *Battle Beyond the Stars*.

QUOTE: *"Hear me, beings of Akir. I am Sador of the Malmori. I have come with my forces to conquer you. If you resist, I will crush you."*

Sark

ORIGIN: ENCOM Corporation computer
SOURCE: *Tron* (1982)

The digital avatar of ENCOM Corporation executive Ed Dillinger, Commander Sark is the principal henchman of the Master Control Program (MCP) that runs the virtual reality video game milieu in 1982's *Tron*. "Brutal and needlessly sadistic" in the words of the MCP itself, Sark is defeated in combat by Tron and "de-rezzed," or destroyed, upon the MCP's demise.

QUOTE: *"Bring in the logic probe."*

SELA

ORIGIN: Planet Romulus
SOURCE: *Star Trek: The Next Generation* (TV series, 1987–1994)

Ruthless, if not particularly competent, female Romulan commander—the product of a forced marriage between the captured human Tasha Yar and a Romulan senator. On *Star Trek: The Next Generation*, Sela's repeated attempts to capture or destroy the starship *Enterprise* are undone by her own tactical blunders.

QUOTE: *"Humans have a way of showing up when you least expect them."*

SOLOMON

ORIGIN: 20th-century Earth
SOURCE: *All-American Comics* #61 (1944)

This name of a wise Biblical king also lends itself to the popular nineteenth-century nursery rhyme "Solomon Grundy," and by extension to the pasty, shambling, brutish DC Comics supervillain Solomon Grundy. Born Cyrus Gold, Grundy is reshaped by mysterious forces into a dimwitted hulk after he is assaulted and left to die in a fetid swamp outside of Gotham City. Reborn in zombified form a century later, Grundy proves impervious to bullets, fire, and extreme cold, and can survive indefinitely without food, water, or oxygen. His sworn enemies include Superman and Green Lantern.

QUOTE: *"Me Solomon Grundy! Me mightier than Superman! Me mightier than all superheroes!"*

TERL

ORIGIN: Planet Psychlo
SOURCE: *Battlefield Earth* (2000)

Ruthless, ambitious head of Psychlo security whose schemes to acquire wealth and power after he is passed over for a promotion drive the plot of the 2000 space epic *Battlefield Earth*. Like all Psychlos, Terl has a low opinion of the "man-animals" whom his people have enslaved.

QUOTE: *"I'm a Psychlo of my word."*

TREVOR

ORIGIN: Bregna
SOURCE: *Aeon Flux* (TV series, 1995)

Trevor Goodchild is the principal antagonist and on-again, off-again lover of the title character on the MTV animated series Aeon Flux. The leader of the nation-state of Bregna, this Trevor is a cold-blooded technocrat who seizes power in a coup d'etat. His chief ambition is consolidating his own power.

QUOTE: *"The will to evil is like an iron in the forge."*

URKO

ORIGIN: Post-apocalyptic Earth
SOURCE: *Planet of the Apes* (TV series, 1974)

A gorilla general on a post-apocalyptic Earth ruled by simians, Urko is the leader of the war-mongering faction in Ape City in the TV version of *Planet of the Apes*. He is apparently no relation to the nearly identical character of Ursus seen in the film *Beneath the Planet of the Apes*.

QUOTE: *"These humans are dangerous. They stir up trouble. They think they're as good as we are."*

URSUS

ORIGIN: Post-apocalyptic Earth
SOURCE: *Beneath the Planet of the Apes* (1970)

A gorilla general on a post-apocalyptic Earth ruled by simians, Ursus is the leader of the war-mongering faction in Ape City in the 1970 feature *Beneath the Planet of the Apes*. With his blustering manner and pathological hatred of humans, backed up by the armed might of legions of thuggish, woofing gorilla shock troops, Ursus becomes a major player on the ape political stage.

QUOTE: *"The only good human is a dead human!"*

VICTOR

ORIGIN: Russia, 11th century B.C.E.
SOURCE: *Highlander* (1986)

Victor Kruger is one of many aliases used by the Kurgan, the power-mad villain of the 1986 sci-fi fantasy epic *Highlander*. A cruel and merciless Immortal from the Russian steppes, the Kurgan is defeated by Connor MacLeod in his fight to claim the Prize, the vaguely described key to universal power.

QUOTE: *"Tonight you sleep in Hell!"*

Vilos

ORIGIN: 21st-century Earth
SOURCE: *Total Recall* (1990)

The villainous chief administrator of Mars in *Total Recall*, Vilos Cohaagen is the mastermind of a sinister conspiracy to deny the planet a breathable atmosphere, thereby maximizing his own power. He is the ultimate example of corporate authority run amok.
QUOTE: *"I'll blow this place up and be home in time for corn-flakes!"*

Vladimir

ORIGIN: Planet Giedi Prime
SOURCE: *Dune* by Frank Herbert (published 1965)

Morbidly obese Baron Vladimir Harkonnen is the head of House Harkonnen and the mortal enemy of House Atreides in Frank Herbert's sci-fi epic *Dune*. A ruthless political operator, the bloated Harkonnen constantly plots to tighten his control over the spice, which, he believes, is the key to universal power.
QUOTE: *"'Revenge.' Has language created a more delicious word?"*

Vlathos

ORIGIN: Unknown
SOURCE: *Teenage Space Vampires* (1998)

Lord Vlathos is an extraterrestrial vampire who travels to Earth, hoping to use the power of his giant diamond to cast the planet into eternal darkness so his people can colonize it in the low-budget 1998 sci-fi shocker *Teenage Space Vampires*.
QUOTE: *"Join us now or you will become a midnight snack for my people."*

Voldar

ORIGIN: Planet Mars
SOURCE: *Santa Claus Conquers the Martians* (1964)

Martian council leader who argues against the Red Planet's planned abduction of Earth icon Santa Claus, on the grounds that Martian children will become soft and frivolous if they laugh and play with toys delivered by the red-suited benefactor. Although depicted as evil, Voldar can be seen as a proud upholder of Mars's warlike heritage.
QUOTE: *"All this trouble over a fat little man in a red suit."*

WEZ

ORIGIN: Future Earth
SOURCE: *The Road Warrior* (1981)

Marauding, mohawked psychopath Wesley Xavier Zonault screams and chews the scenery across a post-apocalyptic Australian wasteland in the 1981 *Mad Max* sequel *The Road Warrior*. Fearless and sadistic, Wez reveals his tender side only in the company of his lover, the Golden Youth.

QUOTE: *"They kill us, we kill them! Kill them! Kill them!"*

YLLANA

ORIGIN: Planet Venus
SOURCE: *Queen of Outer Space* (1958)

Cruel, scarred, man-hating Queen of Venus who schemes to incinerate Planet Earth with a disintegrator ray in the 1958 B-movie *Queen of Outer Space*. She wears a mask to conceal her disfigured face, but cannot hide her evil intentions from her subjects, who plot to overthrow her.

QUOTE: *"I'm going to allow myself the exquisite pleasure of watching you while I obliterate the Earth!"*

ZAIUS

ORIGIN: Post-apocalyptic Earth
SOURCE: *Planet of the Apes* (1968)

Minister of science and chief defender of the faith on a post-apocalyptic Earth ruled by simians, this conniving orangutan (erroneously called a "bloody baboon" by his human captive Taylor) cloaks lies about the true origins of ape society behind his robes of eminence. His hostility to the truth stems from a deep-seated loathing of humans for their role in nearly blowing up the planet, which paved the way for ape ascendancy.

QUOTE: *"Man is a nuisance. The sooner he is exterminated, the better. It's a question of simian survival."*

ZARKON

ORIGIN: Planet Doom
SOURCE: *Voltron: Defender of the Universe* (TV series, 1981–1982)

If your birthplace is Planet Doom, chances are you're going to be a sci-fi supervillain. And if you choose to name your baby after this tyrannical monarch from the animated series *Voltron: Defender of the Universe*, well, you can probably fill in the rest yourself.

QUOTE: *"I've been to the arena many times to see your robotic creations. They cavort about, spew flames, and make hideous sounds. They look evil, but after they fight mighty Voltron you can bring what's left home in a trash can."*

ZARTH

ORIGIN: Unknown
SOURCE: *Starcrash* (1979)

Zarth Arn is the Darth Vader analog (Darth, but with a *Z*, get it?) in the 1979 Italian-made *Star Wars* knockoff *Starcrash*. A cackling, goateed tyrant of satanic mien, he hatches schemes to subjugate the galaxy from his claw-shaped space station redoubt.

QUOTE: *"By sunset I'll be the new emperor. And I'll be the master of the whole universe!"*

ZOD

ORIGIN: 20th-century Earth
SOURCE: *Adventure Comics* #283 (1961)

Maniacal Kryptonian general, banished to the Phantom Zone by the scientist Jor-El for crimes against his home planet. He seeks revenge against the deceased Jor-El's son, Kal-El (a.k.a. Superman), often with the assistance of other Kryptonian prisoners.

QUOTE: *"You will bow down before me, Jor-El. I swear it."*

CHAPTER 5
INTELLECTUAL NAMES

It's time to celebrate the many brilliant scientists, dedicated doctors, and influential thinkers who have populated the realms of sci-fi through the years. If you're looking to raise a future Stephen Hawking or Marie Curie, these are names to consider. But be careful—with the addition of just a few letters (and a fatal character flaw or two) your Einstein could become a Frankenstein.

AEON

ORIGIN: Monica
SOURCE: *Aeon Flux* (TV series, 1995)

Aeon Flux is the titular secret agent from the anarcho-syndicalist state of Monica on the MTV animated series *Aeon Flux*. An amoral Amazon who deals out swift justice to her enemies, the lithe, acrobatic Flux is the free-thinking, free-loving nemesis and sometime paramour of series villain Trevor Goodchild.
QUOTE: *"We won. We must have been right."*

André

ORIGIN: 20th-century Earth
SOURCE: *The Fly* (1958)

Francophile parents can use this French version of Andrew to honor the memory of André Delambre, the devoted scientist, husband, and father whose pioneering teleportation experiments result in his transformation into a repugnant hybrid man/fly in the 1958 version of *The Fly*.
QUOTE: *"Help me! Help meeee!"*

BENDER

ORIGIN: 30th-century Earth
SOURCE: *Futurama* (TV series, 1999–2003)

Bender Bending Rodriguez is the hard-drinking, cigar-smoking robot foil to time-displaced pizza delivery boy Philip J. Fry on the sci-fi cartoon series *Futurama*. His name is an homage by *Futurama* creator Matt Groening to John Bender, the rebellious dirtbag played by Judd Nelson in *The Breakfast Club*.
QUOTE: *"I'm Bender, baby, please insert liquor!"*

BEVERLY

ORIGIN: 24th-century Earth
SOURCE: *Star Trek: The Next Generation* (TV series, 1987–1994)

Choose this Old English place name meaning "beaver stream" if you wish to steer your daughter on the path to a medical career à la Dr. Beverly Crusher, chief medical officer aboard the USS *Enterprise* on *Star Trek: The Next Generation*. A doting single mom, the nurturing, bewigged widow possesses some of the same humanitarian impulses as her predecessor, Leonard McCoy.

QUOTE: *"It's hard to be philosophical when faced with suffering."*

Bruce

ORIGIN: 20th-century Earth
SOURCE: *Incredible Hulk* #1 (Marvel Comics, 1962)
Nuclear physicist Bruce Banner absorbs a blast of gamma rays while working for the U.S. military and emerges as a powerful dark gray (later emerald green) behemoth known as the Hulk. When not in Hulk mode, this Bruce is mild-mannered and analytical, though his transformations can be triggered by the slightest flash of temper.
QUOTE: *"Hulk will smash!"*

Claude

ORIGIN: 20th-century Earth
SOURCE: *Close Encounters of the Third Kind* (1977)
Dogged French UFO researcher Claude Lacombe leads the international team of extraterrestrial experts in *Close Encounters of the Third Kind*. His contention that humans and aliens can converse using musical notes as a language provides the breakthrough that makes first contact a reality.
TRIVIA: *The character of Claude Lacombe is based on real-life French UFO expert Jacques Vallée.*

Cornelius

ORIGIN: Post-apocalyptic Earth
SOURCE: *Planet of the Apes* (1968)
Earnest chimpanzee scientist, devoted husband of Zira, and pioneering explorer of the Forbidden Zone on a post-apocalyptic Earth ruled by simians in the *Planet of the Apes* film series. A skeptical archaeologist, Cornelius ignores conventional wisdom and recognizes the intelligence and dignity of human prisoners.
QUOTE: *"Flight is a scientific impossibility!"*

Emmett

ORIGIN: 20th-century Earth
SOURCE: *Back to the Future* (1985)
Little-used first name of Emmett "Doc" Brown, a daffy but brilliant inventor who constructs a time machine out of a DeLorean sports car and sends his teenage friend Marty McFly hurtling back

in time to the 1950s in *Back to the Future.*

QUOTE: *"There's that word again—'heavy.' Why are things so heavy in the future? Is there a problem with the Earth's gravitational pull?"*

Gazoo

ORIGIN: Planet Zatox
SOURCE: *The Flintstones* (TV series, 1999–2003)

This tiny green alien from the planet Zatox drops into the lives of Stone Age laborers Fred Flintstone and Barney Rubble on the animated TV series *The Flintstones.* A supercilious imp who appears to have dominion over all matter, "The Great" Gazoo attempts to help the dull-witted cavemen improve their lots in life, but invariably sees his good intentions go comically awry.

QUOTE: *"Toodle-oo, dum dums!"*

Genius

ORIGIN: 20th-century Earth
SOURCE: *Village of the Giants* (1965)

Boy, well, genius whose invention of a secret concoction designed to make animals grow leads to unintended consequences of the colossal teenager variety in the 1965 sci-fi drive-in feature *Village of the Giants.* An idealist, Genius hopes his "goo" will solve the world's food shortage, but like a lot of geniuses, his humanitarian vision is exploited by opportunistic older kids.

QUOTE: *"Kiddo? I prefer to be called Genius, if you don't mind."*

Geordi

ORIGIN: 24th-century Earth
SOURCE: *Star Trek: The Next Generation* (TV series, 1987–1994)

The redoubtable blind chief engineer of the USS *Enterprise*-D on *Star Trek: The Next Generation,* Lieutenant Commander Geordi LaForge outpaces even his predecessor, Montgomery Scott, in his ability to diagnose and solve the myriad catastrophes that beset a Galaxy-class starship. As wonkishly well-versed as Geordi is in his ship's systems, however, he is clueless when it comes to the mechanics of the human heart.

QUOTE: *"There's theory . . . and then there's application. They don't always jibe."*

HAL

ORIGIN: H.A.L. plant, Urbana, Illinois, 1992
SOURCE: *2001: A Space Odyssey* (1968)

Homicidal supercomputer, famed for its reliability, in the book and film *2001*. HAL stands for Heuristic Algorithmic Computer, although incrementing each letter of HAL by one spells out "IBM." Full name: HAL 9000.

QUOTE: *"I am putting myself to the fullest possible use, which is all I think that any conscious entity can ever hope to do."*

OTHER NOTABLE SCI-FI HALS: *Hal Jordan (Silver Age Green Lantern)*

Hans

ORIGIN: 20th-century Earth
SOURCE: *Flash Gordon* comic strip (1934)

Brilliant scientist Hans Zarkov builds a rocket ship and accompanies Flash Gordon and Dale Arden on their journey to the planet Mongo. His scientific insights often prove invaluable to the trio as they fight off the threat posed by the tyrannical Ming the Merciless.

QUOTE: *"We are interested in friendship. Why do you attack us?"*

Harold

ORIGIN: 20th-century Earth
SOURCE: *Them!* (1954)

Oracular Department of Agriculture entomologist Harold Medford correctly surmises that common household ants are being mutated to colossal size by radiation from a nearby nuclear test site in the 1954 giant bug epic *Them!*

QUOTE: *"We may be witnessing a Biblical prophecy come true."*

Helena

ORIGIN: 20th-century Earth
SOURCE: *Space: 1999* (TV series, 1975–1977)

Beautiful, brainy Dr. Helena Russell, the chief of the Moonbase Alpha medical section, is the ultimate combination of intellect and beauty. The daughter of a prominent physician, Helena occasionally finds time away from her medical responsibilities to pursue her other passion, holographic sculpture.

QUOTE: *"Our brains are such incredible instruments. Just think what we might be able to achieve if we knew how to use them to their fullest potential."*

HEYWOOD

ORIGIN: 21st-century Earth
SOURCE: *2001: A Space Odyssey* (1968)

Influential scientist Heywood R. Floyd appears in *2001: A Space Odyssey* and several subsequent iterations of author Arthur C. Clarke's *Space Odyssey* series. He is best known for authorizing the 2001 mission to Jupiter to investigate the appearance of a mysterious monolith that sets the events of the film in motion.

QUOTE: *"Someday, the children of the new sun will meet the children of the old. I think they will be our friends."*

HOLLY

ORIGIN: Mining ship *Red Dwarf*
SOURCE: *Red Dwarf* (BBC TV series, 1988–1999)

The superintelligent supercomputer who runs the systems aboard the mining ship *Red Dwarf*, Holly possesses an IQ of 6,000 and appears in its viewscreen interface as a disembodied human head, alternately male and female.

QUOTE: *"It's a mistake any deranged, half-witted computer coulda made."*

JACOB

ORIGIN: 20th-century Earth
SOURCE: *The Day the Earth Stood Still* (1951)

Choose this Biblically inspired name to honor a man of science with a global conscience: renowned scientist Dr. Jacob Barnhardt, who counsels the alien emissary Klaatu on how best to deliver his message of world peace to heedless Earth leaders in the 1951 sci-fi classic *The Day the Earth Stood Still*.

QUOTE: *"It isn't faith that makes good science, Mr. Klaatu. It's curiosity."*

JEREMY

ORIGIN: 20th-century Earth
SOURCE: *The Andromeda Strain* (1971)

Nobel Prize–winning professor of bacteriology Jeremy Stone leads the team of scientists searching for a cure to a deadly virus in the 1971 film *The Andromeda Strain*. He's a focused taskmaster with a "by the book" approach to solving problems.

QUOTE: *"Stick to established procedures."*

JULIAN

ORIGIN: 24th-century Earth

SOURCE: *Star Trek: Deep Space Nine* (TV series, 1993–1999)

Patients will be in good hands if you raise a doctor named after this *Star Trek: Deep Space Nine* medicine mensch. The space station's chief medical officer, Julian "Jules" Bashir is a product of genetic engineering in childhood. His enhanced mental capacity does not deter him from jumping at the chance to practice "real frontier medicine" on Deep Space Nine.

QUOTE: *"I'm a doctor. You're my patient. That's all I need to know."*

KARL

ORIGIN: 20th-century Earth

SOURCE: *Attack of the Crab Monsters* (1957)

Nuclear physicist Karl Weigand leads a group of scientists to a remote Pacific island inhabited by giant, atomically mutated crabs in the 1957 B-movie *Attack of the Crab Monsters*. He is one of the first to suspect the presence of mutations and the last to be eaten by them.

QUOTE: *"We are unquestionably on the brink of a great discovery. It is not likely that that discovery will be of a pleasant nature."*

KATE

ORIGIN: 24th-century Earth

SOURCE: *Star Trek: The Next Generation* (TV series, 1987–1994)

Short form of Katherine employed by Dr. Kate Pulaski, a one-season wonder aboard the USS *Enterprise* under Captain Jean-Luc Picard. Earthy and opinionated, this Kate shares some of her predecessor Leonard McCoy's suspicion of machines and predilection for dispensing old-time moralistic bromides.

QUOTE: *"Haven't we grown beyond the point where we resolve our problems with physical conflict?"*

KERR

ORIGIN: Future Earth

SOURCE: *Blake's Seven* (BBC TV series, 1978–1981)

Caustic computer genius who serves as the Dr. McCoy to Roj Blake's Captain Kirk on the BBC sci-fi series *Blake's Seven*. As cynical as Blake is idealistic, Kerr joins the anti-Federation resistance for his own self-serving reasons. He eventually supplants Blake as leader of the "Seven."

QUOTE: *"Profound philosophical questions never interested me."*

Leonard

ORIGIN: 23rd-century Earth
SOURCE: *Star Trek* (TV series, 1966–1969)
Irascible chief medical officer Dr. Leonard McCoy is the conscience of the starship *Enterprise*, a julep-sipping old-time country doctor whose nickname, "Bones," derives from the ancient Earth term *sawbones* for physician.

QUOTE: *"I'm a doctor, not a bricklayer!"*

Leopold

ORIGIN: 20th-century Earth
SOURCE: *Night of the Lepus* (1972)
Arizona forensics expert who investigates a series of mysterious gnawing deaths in the 1972 mutant bunny shocker *Night of the Lepus*. For a man of science, Leopold is unusually eager to look for causes not found in the natural world—entertaining the possibility of vampires and saber-tooth tigers before settling on the real culprits, a horde of giant carnivorous rabbits.

QUOTE: *"In the smallest of objects, one can find a world of discovery."*

Liz

ORIGIN: 20th-century Earth
SOURCE: *Dr. Who* (BBC TV series, 1963–present)
Short form of Elizabeth preferred by Liz Shaw, a scientific advisor to Brigadier Alistair Lethbridge Stewart who assists the third regeneration of the Time Lord known as the Doctor during his period of exile on Earth.

TRIVIA: *Liz Shaw is the only one of the Doctor's companions never to travel aboard the TARDIS.*

Marion

ORIGIN: 20th-century Earth
SOURCE: *Outland* (1981)

Hoping to raise a future lady doc who combines some of Leonard McCoy's crusty humanism with the tart tongue of Dr. Kate Pulaski? Try naming your child after Marion Lazarus, the flinty chief medical officer at a remote mining colony on one of Jupiter's moons in the 1981 Sean Connery starrer *Outland*.

QUOTE: *"Take two aspirin and call me in the morning. That's a doctor joke."*

NED

ORIGIN: 20th-century Earth
SOURCE: *The Absent-Minded Professor* (1961)

Not all great scientists invent androids or rocket ships. To fix your brainchild's sights on more prosaic goals, try naming him after the inventor of the miraculous rubber known as Flubber, Ned Brainard (see, even his last name says "smarts").

QUOTE: *"Let's see, flying rubber . . . Flubber!"*

OLIVER

ORIGIN: 19th-century Earth
SOURCE: *Journey to the Center of the Earth* (1959)

Instill a zest for geologic inquiry into your male child by naming him after Professor Oliver Lindenbrook, the Scottish scientist who leads an expedition to the Earth's molten core in the 1959 sci-fi adventure *Journey to the Center of the Earth*.

QUOTE: *"A scientist who cannot prove what he has accomplished has accomplished nothing."*

REED

ORIGIN: 20th-century Earth
SOURCE: *Fantastic Four* #1 (Marvel Comics, 1961)

Scientist and inventor Reed Richards is transformed into the super-elongated superhero Mister Fantastic when he and three colleagues are bombarded with cosmic rays during a rocket ship test flight. Widely regarded as one of the world's smartest men, Reed employs an analytical approach to solving problems.

QUOTE: *"Sometimes there's no improving on the original concept."*

RODNEY

ORIGIN: Planet Earth

SOURCE: *Stargate Atlantis* (TV series, 2004–present)

Want to raise a future Mensa member? Then name your son after Rodney McKay, the acerbic Canadian astrophysicist and genius-society inductee who serves as chief scientific advisor to the Stargate Atlantis team on the TV series *Stargate Atlantis*.

QUOTE: *"I'm sorry, medicine is about as much of a science as . . . uh, oh, I don't know, voodoo?"*

RUDY

ORIGIN: 20th-century Earth

SOURCE: *The Six Million Dollar Man* (TV series, 1974–1978)

Rudy Wells is the head of the bionics team on *The Six Million Dollar Man*. Brilliant and innovative, he helps save the lives of both astronaut Steve Austin and tennis star Jaime Sommers by replacing their injured body parts with superpowered electro-mechanical devices.

QUOTE: *"I want to show you something, Steve. This is your arm."*

SAMUEL

ORIGIN: 23rd-century Earth

SOURCE: *X: The Man with the X-Ray Eyes* (1963)

Hoping to raise a future eye doctor? Then name your son after one of cinema's true men of vision, Dr. Samuel Brandt, the avuncular ophthalmologist who tries to talk his friend Dr. James Xavier out of testing an experimental X-ray vision formula on himself in the 1963 cult classic *X: The Man with the X-Ray Eyes*.

QUOTE: *"Only the gods see everything."*

OTHER NOTABLE SCI-FI SAMUELS: *Sam Beckett (*Quantum Leap *protagonist)*

SANTEE

ORIGIN: 20th-century Earth

SOURCE: *Day of the Animals* (1977)

We include this Native American name (meaning "knife") to honor not Western "intellect," but the wisdom of indigenous elders like Daniel Santee, the oracular Indian tracker who divines the coming revolt of Earth's creatures as a result of the depleted ozone layer in the alarmist 1977 feature *Day of the Animals*.

QUOTE: *"There's something strange in the woods and I don't know what it is."*

SCOTTY

ORIGIN: 23rd-century Earth
SOURCE: *Star Trek* (TV series, 1966–1969)

The redoubtable chief engineer of the starship *Enterprise*, Montgomery "Scotty" Scott saves the ship from imminent destruction on numerous occasions, using a combination of technical proficiency and good old-fashioned Highland horse sense. A two-fisted drinker and accomplished bagpiper, Scotty is a man of many talents and passions.

QUOTE: *"I can't change the laws of physics! I've got to have thirty minutes!"*

Sebastian

ORIGIN: 20th-century Earth
SOURCE: *Hollow Man* (2000)

Brilliant, Twinkie-loving scientist Sebastian Kane discovers the secret of invisibility in 2000's *Hollow Man*, but like many of his fellow eccentric visionaries he neglects to account for his revolutionary formula's unpleasant side effects. A descent into homicidal madness ensues.

QUOTE: *"Ghosts are dead. I'm very much alive."*

Seth

ORIGIN: 20th-century Earth
SOURCE: *The Fly* (1986)

Be afraid. Be very afraid of what you may find lying in your crib one morning if you name your child after eccentric scientist Seth Brundle, the unfortunate lead character of the 1986 version of *The Fly*. Transformed by his own teleportation experiments into a man-sized housefly, Brundle is the epitome of the driven, obsessive scientist gone awry.

QUOTE: *"I was not pure. The teleporter insists on inner pure."*

SiGMUND

ORIGIN: 20th-century Earth
SOURCE: *The Bees* (1978)

If you want to put your unborn son on the fast track to a career in apiology, consider naming him after Dr. Sigmund Hummel, an eminent bee expert whose thick German accent proves to be no protection against a mutant swarm of killer bees in the alarmist 1978 insect invasion feature *The Bees*.

QUOTE: *"Zey know everyting! Zey are tinking bees!"*

SPOCK

ORIGIN: Planet Vulcan
SOURCE: *Star Trek* (TV series, 1966–1969)

His Vulcan birth name is unpronounceable, so the world knows this legendary half-human, half-Vulcan science officer only as Spock. Cool and analytical, with a rigorously logical mind and prodigious intellect, Captain Kirk's indispensable first officer slips up only when his suppressed human emotions bubble to the surface—or when he finds himself in the grip of the maddening Vulcan mating fever known as *pon farr*.

QUOTE: *"Fascinating!"*

SUrAK

ORIGIN: Planet Vulcan
SOURCE: *Star Trek* (TV series, 1966–1969)

Not to be confused with Sarek, Surak is the father of the Vulcan philosophy of absolute logic and a titanic figure in the history of intergalactic thought. His teachings helped lead the Vulcans out of barbarism and ushered in an era of peace and enlightenment.

QUOTE: *"May we together become greater than the sum of both of us."*

THUrGOOD

ORIGIN: 20th-century Earth
SOURCE: *The Beast from 20,000 Fathoms* (1953)

Sure, you could name your son after Thurgood Marshall, the legendary Supreme Court justice. But that would be too obvious. Better to name him after Professor Thurgood Elson, the world-renowned paleontologist in the 1953 B-feature *The Beast from 20,000 Fathoms*.

QUOTE: *"This is such a strange feeling, I feel as though I'm leaving a world of untold tomorrows for a world of countless yesterdays."*

TONY

ORIGIN: 20th-century Earth
SOURCE: *Tales of Suspense* #39 (Marvel Comics, 1963)
Tony Stark is not only one of the world's wealthiest industrialists, he's also one of the world's smartest men, having gained entrance to MIT at age 15 and graduated at the top of his class. He puts his intellect to good use by designing an impregnable suit of iron body armor and fighting America's enemies as Iron Man.
QUOTE: *"My brain still thinks! My heart still beats! But in order to remain alive I must spend the rest of my life in this iron prison!"*
VARIANTS: *Anthony*
OTHER NOTABLE SCI-FI TONYS: *Tony Verdeschi (Moonbase Alpha's security chief,* Space: 1999*)*

Victor

ORIGIN: 20th-century Earth
SOURCE: *Space: 1999* (TV series, 1975–1977)
An astronomer with a philosophical bent, Dr. Victor Bergman serves as chief scientist on Moonbase Alpha on *Space: 1999*. A balding fiftysomething with enormous sideburns, Victor is in charge of maintaining Moonbase Alpha's artificial gravity systems.
QUOTE: *"Maybe I've had enough of Earth and its so-called civilization."*
OTHER SCI-FI VICTORS: *Victor Doom (Marvel Comics supervillain)*

Vril

ORIGIN: Planet Bryak
SOURCE: *Action Comics* #242 (1958)
Want to raise a real brainiac? Then choose the birth name of Brainiac, the cerebrally supercharged Superman nemesis born Vril Dox on the planet Bryak. Unfortunately, Vril's prodigious intellect is matched only by his extreme megalomania and ethical vacuity, so be vigilant lest your child end up in jail rather than in Stockholm accepting the Nobel Prize.
QUOTE: *"Farewell, boy! Share the fate of any who think they can stand against the great Brainiac!"*

Zapp

ORIGIN: 30th-century Earth
SOURCE: *Futurama* (TV series, 1999–2003)

Conceited, cocksure space jockey General Major Webelo "Zapp" Brannigan commands the starship *Nimbus* on the TV sci-fi cartoon series *Futurama*. An incorrigible braggart and self-styled ladies' man, Brannigan may have been modeled after the character of Captain Kirk from *Star Trek*, though his initials also suggest an homage to Zaphod Beeblebrox of *The Hitchhiker's Guide to the Galaxy*.

QUOTE: *"I am the man with no name—Zapp Brannigan—at your service."*

Zira

ORIGIN: Post-apocalyptic Earth
SOURCE: *Planet of the Apes* (1968)

This concerned animal biologist, wife of Cornelius, befriends the captured human Taylor after his time-traveling spacecraft washes up on the shores of a future Earth ruled by simians in *Planet of the Apes*. A humanitarian in every sense of the world, this brilliant and caring chimpanzee fights against the creeping militarism and distrust of science ascendant in Ape City.

QUOTE: *"Gorillas are cruel because they're stupid! All bone and no brain!"*

CHAPTER 6

EXOTIC NAMES

With more and more ordinary parents choosing unconventional names for baby, it's clear that bizarre handles aren't just for celebrities anymore. Sure, Moon Unit's cool, but it's played, son, so where better to look for truly distinctive *and* impractical name ideas than the out-of-this-world realms of science fiction? Here are some enduring favorites. Bestow them at your own—or really, your child's—risk.

ABRAXAS

ORIGIN: Planet Sargacia
SOURCE: *Abraxas, Guardian of the Universe* (1991)

The name of a deity worshipped by a second-century Gnostic sect, Abraxas has a completely different meaning for fans of cheaply produced early 1990s Canadian sci-fi. It is the name of the intergalactic policeman (played by future Minnesota governor Jesse Ventura) who comes to Earth to apprehend his renegade former partner in the 1991 space adventure *Abraxas, Guardian of the Universe.*

QUOTE: *"You will speak when spoken to or I will deactivate your vocal mode!"*

AKTON

ORIGIN: Unknown
SOURCE: *Starcrash* (1979)

Looking for an alternative to Obi-Wan? So were a lot of people in 1979. This superpowered alien starship navigator from that year's Italian-made *Star Wars* knockoff *Starcrash* has a lot of the same crypto-mystical attributes as the elderly Jedi, but in a younger, groovier, disco-era package, highlighted by an enormous, unruly blonde afro.

QUOTE: *"You would have tried to change the future, which is against the law. So therefore I can tell you nothing."*

AMIDALA

ORIGIN: Planet Naboo
SOURCE: *Star Wars: The Phantom Menace* (1999)

Also known as Padmé Amidala, Queen Amidala of Naboo plays a critical role in the foundation of the Rebel Alliance in the early installments of George Lucas's *Star Wars* saga. A ravishing beauty with a saturnine disposition and a reputation for being headstrong, she is a voice of moderation and reason as Naboo's representative in the Galactic Senate.

QUOTE: *"If we do not act quickly, all will be lost forever."*

ANAKIN

ORIGIN: Planet Tattooine
SOURCE: *Star Wars: The Phantom Menace* (1999)

Strong in the Force, Tattooine native Anakin Skywalker becomes apprenticed to the Jedi Master Obi-Wan Kenobi. He is tempted over to the Dark Side by the villainous Chancellor Palpatine, however, and eventually dons the ghastly garb of a Sith Lord, rechristening himself as the cruel, black-armored warrior Darth Vader.

QUOTE: *"Something's happening. I'm not the Jedi I should be."*

Arex

ORIGIN: Planet Edos
SOURCE: *Star Trek: The Animated Series* (TV series, 1973–1974)

Brick-colored tripodal alien from the planet Edos who serves as navigator of the starship *Enterprise* on *Star Trek: The Animated Series.* Known for his lightning-quick reflexes, Arex leads a solitary existence when away from his post.

TRIVIA: *Because he has three arms and three legs, Arex must have his Starfleet uniforms specially tailored.*

Barbarella

ORIGIN: Unknown
SOURCE: *Barbarella* (1968)

The French comic book heroine Barbarella has been called "the female James Bond" for her resourcefulness and implacability in the most dangerous situations. This courageous space traveler combines over-the-top feminine sex appeal with butt-kicking attitude.

QUOTE: *"A good many dramatic situations begin with screaming."*

Beldar

ORIGIN: Planet Remulak
SOURCE: *Saturday Night Live* (TV series, 1975–present)

The patriarch of a family of extraterrestrial "Coneheads" residing in the suburban United States. Despite his cone-shaped head, monotone speech patterns, and voracious eating habits, Beldar has little trouble passing as an immigrant from France.

QUOTE: *"If I did not fear incarceration from human authority figures, I would terminate your life functions by applying sufficient pressure to your blunt skull so as to force its collapse!"*

Benton

ORIGIN: 20th-century Earth
SOURCE: *Jonny Quest* (TV series, 1964–1965)

Dr. Benton Quest is a brilliant scientist, doting paterfamilias, and resourceful team leader on the animated sci-fi adventure series *Jonny Quest*. The birth father of Jonny and adopted sire of Hadji Singh, the widowed Quest travels the globe investigating scientific mysteries.

QUOTE: *"Now, now, Dreena, keep your courage up."*

Boba

ORIGIN: Planet Kamino
SOURCE: *The Empire Strikes Back* (1980)

Notorious bounty hunter Boba Fett hails from the planet Kamino, where he was raised as the natural-born son of his clone progenitor, Jango Fett. Famous for his ruthlessness in pursuing (and often disintegrating) his prey, Boba is hired by Darth Vader to track down Han Solo and the crew of the *Millennium Falcon* in the fifth episode of George Lucas's *Star Wars* saga.

QUOTE: *"He's no good to me dead."*

Buckaroo

ORIGIN: 20th-century
SOURCE: *The Adventures of Buckaroo Banzai Across the 8th Dimension* (1984)

If you're envisioning a life full of adventure for your son, you can do no better than naming him after this multitalented action hero, neurosurgeon, particle physicist, race-car driver, rock star, and last bastion of hope for humanity.

QUOTE: *"No matter where you go, there you are."*

Cayman

ORIGIN: Lambda Zone
SOURCE: *Battle Beyond the Stars* (1980)

Cayman is the name of both an idyllic island destination in the Caribbean and of Cayman of the Lambda Zone, the last survivor of the Lazuli, a lizardlike alien race destroyed by the evil Sador of Malmori in the 1980 B-movie *Battle Beyond the Stars*.

QUOTE: *"Turn around, you over-aged degenerate, and we'll bump heads!"*

CHAKOTAY

ORIGIN: 24th-century Earth
SOURCE: *Star Trek: Voyager* (TV series, 1995–2001)

A Native American of the fictional Anurabi tribe, this *Star Trek: Voyager* officer's mononym means "earth-walking man" in his native language. At first a rival to Captain Janeway's authority, Chakotay grows into her most trusted confidant.

QUOTE: *"I've found that when you don't think about a problem . . . sometimes the solution comes to you."*

CHEWBACCA

ORIGIN: Planet Kashyyyk
SOURCE: *Star Wars* (1977)

"Chewie" for short, Chewbacca is Han Solo's shambling, Sasquatch-like Wookiee sidekick in George Lucas's *Star Wars* saga. An indispensable copilot of the *Millennium Falcon*, Chewbacca more than compensates for his less than sparkling conversational skills (he speaks chiefly in an ursine roar) with his in-depth knowledge of ship's systems and technology.

TRIVIA: *Chewbacca has a wife, Mallatobuck, and a son, Lumpawarrump.*

CLU

ORIGIN: ENCOM Corporation
SOURCE: *Tron* (1982)

Colorful digital avatar of computer programming whiz Kevin Flynn in the video-game world depicted in the 1982 film *Tron*. The flesh-and-blood Flynn assumes the form of the electronic gladiator (named for one of the programs he designed) after he is zapped by a laser wielded by the artificial intelligence known as the Master Control Program.

QUOTE: *"Forget it, mister high-and-mighty Master Control! You're not going to make me talk!"*

DATA

ORIGIN: Planet Omicron Theta
SOURCE: *Star Trek: The Next Generation* (TV series, 1987–1994)

Pasty-faced, yellow-eyed android Lieutenant Commander Data mans the "ops" station aboard the USS *Enterprise*-D on *Star*

Trek: The Next Generation. A "fully functional" human simulacrum with an immensely powerful positronic brain, Data differs from the real thing in a key respect: He cannot feel emotions, a deficiency he works his entire lifespan to overcome.

QUOTE: *"If you prick me, do I not leak?"*

DELENN

ORIGIN: Planet Minbar
SOURCE: *Babylon 5* (TV series, 1994–1998)

Delenn is the Minbari ambassador, sent to space station Babylon 5 to monitor the activity of senior military officer Jeffrey Sinclair, on the TV space opera *Babylon 5*. She is known for her wisdom and moral rectitude.

QUOTE: *"Now we make our own magic. Now we create our own legends. Now we build the future."*

DIM

ORIGIN: Future Earth
SOURCE: *A Clockwork Orange* (1971)

A fine example of a name that perfectly describes the person on whom it was bestowed, Dim memorializes the unforgettable halfwitted "droog" who turns on his reformed friend Alexander de Large in Stanley Kubrick's *A Clockwork Orange*. Fat, pasty, and stupid, Dim betters his own lot by forsaking a life of petty crime for a rewarding career in law enforcement.

QUOTE: *"Yarbles! Great bolshy yarblockos to you."*

DROPO

ORIGIN: Planet Mars
SOURCE: *Santa Claus Conquers the Martians* (1964)

This dimwitted Martian prole, the so-called "laziest man on Mars," is inexplicably tapped to take part in a mission to Earth to abduct Kris Kringle in the 1964 Christmas-themed sci-fi feature *Santa Claus Conquers the Martians*.

QUOTE: *"It's just that I haven't been able to sleep these last few months. I forgot how."*

GAFF

ORIGIN: 21st-century Earth
SOURCE: *Blade Runner* (1982)

Mysterious, origami-obsessed LAPD official who shadows Rick Deckard's every move in Ridley Scott's noir sci-fi classic *Blade Runner*. He communicates with Deckard using a combination of futuristic hipster argot called Cityspeak and the intricately folded animal figures he leaves behind as "clues."

QUOTE: *"It's too bad she won't live! But then again, who does?"*

GELT

ORIGIN: Unknown
SOURCE: *Battle Beyond the Stars* (1980)

Laconic mercenary Gelt puts aside his crushing ennui (and his massive personal fortune) long enough to join the band of guns-for-hire who help the peaceful people of Akir liberate themselves from the oppressive rule of the tyrannical Sador in the 1980 B-movie space opera *Battle Beyond the Stars*.

QUOTE: *"I sleep with my back to the wall, when I can sleep. I eat serpents, seven times a week. There's not a major city in this galaxy where I can show my face or spend my wealth."*

GUINAN

ORIGIN: Planet El-Auria
SOURCE: *Star Trek: The Next Generation* (TV series, 1987–1994)

This mysterious, headdress-bedecked barmaid dispenses gnomic snippets of wisdom along with mind-altering libations.

TRIVIA: *The character of Guinan was named after famed actress and saloonkeeper Mary Louise Cecilia "Texas" Guinan.*

HUBERT

ORIGIN: 29th-century Earth
SOURCE: *Futurama* (TV series, 1999–2003)

Elderly mad scientist Hubert J. Farnsworth is the employer and only surviving relative of time-traveling pizza delivery boy Philip J. Fry on the sci-fi cartoon series *Futurama*. Callous and demented, Professor Farnsworth often leads his charges on seemingly suicidal missions in pursuit of his selfish pseudo-scientific goals.

QUOTE: *"Dirt doesn't need luck!"*

Ian

ORIGIN: 20th-century Earth
SOURCE: *Jurassic Park* (1993)

Choose this distinctive Scottish variant of John to honor prescient mathematician Dr. Ian Malcolm, a gangly proponent of chaos theory who is among the first to express misgivings about the dinosaur theme park being constructed by wealthy entrepreneur John Hammond in the 1993 sci-fi monster fest *Jurassic Park*.

QUOTE: *"I'm fairly alarmed here."*

Jabba

ORIGIN: Planet Nal Hutta
SOURCE: *The Return of the Jedi* (1983)

Known familiarly as Jabba the Hutt, the revolting alien crimelord Jabba Desilijic Tiure hails from the Hutt race, a species of fat, indolent, sluglike, hermaphrodite hedonists who delight in the suffering and enslavement of others. Exemplary even among the Hutts for his depravity, Jabba holds Han Solo captive in the sixth installment of George Lucas's *Star Wars* saga.

QUOTE: *"This bounty hunter is my kind of scum: fearless and inventive."*

Jar-Jar

ORIGIN: Planet Naboo
SOURCE: *Star Wars: The Phantom Menace* (1999)

Gangly, shambling Gungan whose progressively diminished roles in the first three installments of the *Star Wars* saga reflect the low esteem in which he is held by fans of the film series. Naïve and trusting, the blithering Jar-Jar inadvertently plays a key role in the rise of Emperor Palpatine.

QUOTE: *"Yoosa should follow me now, okeeday?"*

Jor-El

ORIGIN: Planet Krypton
SOURCE: *Action Comics* #1 (1938)

Respected Kryptonian scientist who tries unsuccessfully to warn his colleagues about the planet's impending destruction in *Superman* comics. A paragon of self-sacrifice, Jor-El allows himself and his wife to perish so that he can send his infant son Kal-El to Earth in a homemade rocket ship.

KLaatu

ORIGIN: Unknown
SOURCE: *The Day the Earth Stood Still* (1951)

Suave alien ambassador who visits Earth on a mission of peace in the 1951 sci-fi classic *The Day the Earth Stood Still*. Frustrated by the squabbling he observes among Earth's world leaders (and briefly inconvenienced by a jittery soldier's bullet), Klaatu must ultimately resort to a show of force in order to convince the planet's inhabitants to choose peace over war.

QUOTE: *"I'm impatient when I encounter stupidity. My people have learned to live without it."*

Kurn

ORIGIN: Planet Kronos
SOURCE: *Star Trek: The Next Generation* (TV series, 1987–1994)

Kurn is the impulsive younger brother of Worf, son of Mogh, on *Star Trek: The Next Generation*. He urges his sibling to join forces with him in a campaign to restore the good name of their disgraced father.

QUOTE: *"The time for glory is here. It is not a time to worry about stabilizers. It is a time to celebrate, for tomorrow, we all may die!"*

Lennier

ORIGIN: Planet Minbar
SOURCE: *Babylon 5* (TV series, 1994–1998)

Lennier is the faithful diplomatic aide to Minbari ambassador Delenn on *Babylon 5*. Fresh out of a monastery and lacking real-world experience, Lennier nevertheless masters the art of diplomacy and grows so unswerving in his loyalty to Delenn that his own judgment often becomes clouded.

QUOTE: *"A darkness carried in the heart cannot be cured by moving the body from one place to another."*

LONDO

ORIGIN: Planet Centauri Prime
SOURCE: *Babylon 5* (TV series, 1994–1998)

The Centauri ambassador to space station Babylon 5, Londo Mollari is known for his quick wit, easy charm, and willingness to use whatever means are at his disposal to advance his agenda and achieve his goals.

QUOTE: *"There comes a time when you look into the mirror and realize that what you see is all that you will ever be."*

MOONPIE

ORIGIN: 21st-century Earth
SOURCE: *Rollerball* (1975)

Distinctive moniker, possibly a nickname, used by one of the superstars of Rollerball, a violent sport played in Earth's dystopian near future.

QUOTE: *"We're livin' good. You know we are."*

M'RESS

ORIGIN: Planet Cait
SOURCE: *Star Trek: The Animated Series* (TV series, 1973–1974)

The catlike alien communications officer aboard the USS *Enterprise* on *Star Trek: The Animated Series*, M'Ress is a Caitian female, distinguished by her luxurious orange mane, yellow eyes, and purring voice.

TRIVIA: *Due to the thick pads on her paws, M'Ress does not need to wear shoes.*

NAMOR

ORIGIN: Kingdom of Atlantis
SOURCE: *Marvel Comics* #1 (1939)

If you've already used Orin (see p. 59) to instill a love of the sea in your male offspring, then consider this name of Aquaman's Marvel Comics counterpart. The valiant, regal Prince of Atlantis, Namor the Sub-Mariner combines super strength with unmatched swimming ability and an uncanny dominion over all marine life.

QUOTE: *"I am Supreme Monarch of the realm eternal!"*

neelix

ORIGIN: Planet Talax
SOURCE: *Star Trek: Voyager* (TV series, 1995–2001)

Culinary school may be in the cards for the child named after this Talaxian who endeavors to master the lost art of cooking on *Star Trek: Voyager*. Though he proves an able chef in an age of replicated food, Neelix eventually forsakes the kitchen for a second career in diplomacy.

QUOTE: *"Waste nothing. That's one of the first rules of survival."*

neo

ORIGIN: The Matrix
SOURCE: *The Matrix* (1999)

Next to Luke Skywalker, perhaps the most revered hero in contemporary sci-fi is this stolid *Matrix* protagonist. A messiah in cool shades in an illusory recreation of twentieth-century Earth—designed by aliens to prevent the planet's inhabitants from apprehending that their world is now little more than a large battery—Neo is an anagram for "One," the name by which he is heralded in Matrix mythology.

QUOTE: *"I don't like the idea that I'm not in control of my life."*

norrin

ORIGIN: Planet Zenn-La
SOURCE: *Fantastic Four* #48 (Marvel Comics, 1966)

A terrific name for rebels, dreamers, and questing souls, Norrin Radd is the birth name of the Silver Surfer, a disillusioned astronomer from the planet Zenn-La who saves his home world from consumption by the cosmic glutton Galactus by agreeing to become his herald.

QUOTE: *"These are not ants, master. They think! They feel!"*

obi-wan

ORIGIN: Unknown
SOURCE: *Star Wars* (1977)

Raised from childhood to be a Jedi Knight, Obi-Wan Kenobi studied under two of the greatest Jedi Masters, Yoda and Qui-Gon Jinn. Although devastated by the loss of his own star pupil, Anakin Skywalker, to the Dark Side, he redeems himself by training Anakin's son, Luke Skywalker, in the ways of the Jedi. A paragon of self-sacrifice and a font of wisdom whether in corporeal or spiritual form, Obi-Wan is one of the most beloved figures in the *Star Wars* mythos. Also known as Ben Kenobi.

QUOTE: *"In my experience, there's no such thing as luck."*

ODO

ORIGIN: Changeling planet
SOURCE: *Star Trek: Deep Space Nine* (TV series, 1993–1999)

The shape-shifting Constable Odo serves as security chief aboard space station Deep Space Nine on TV's *Star Trek: Deep Space Nine*. A space traveler rescued by the Bajorans while in his naturally gelatinous form, he is given the full name Odo'ital—or "nothing."

QUOTE: *"Laws change depending on who's making them . . . but justice is justice."*

Panic

ORIGIN: 20th-century Earth
SOURCE: *Ticks* (1994)

Self-assured teenage gang-banger Darrel "Panic" Lumley sees his excursion into the woods with a group of fellow at-risk youths interrupted by the emergence of a horde of softball-sized mutant arachnids in the 1994 sci-fi shocker *Ticks*.

QUOTE: *"See, they call me Panic 'cause I never do."*

PLUTHAR

ORIGIN: Planet Pluton
SOURCE: *TerrorVision* (1986)

"Sanitation captain" from the planet Pluton who attempts to warn the people of Earth that a ravenous Plutonian pet beamed into space from his waste disposal station may be headed for their world via satellite television signal in the low-budget 1986 shocker *TerrorVision*.

QUOTE: *"A stray energy beam from my substation may be headed for your solar system and could possibly result in the total annihilation of your species. I'm so terribly sorry for the inconvenience."*

Pris

ORIGIN: 21st-century Earth
SOURCE: *Blade Runner* (1982)

"Pleasure model" replicant in a dystopian future Los Angeles in which the artificial life forms are hunted down and terminated. Beautiful and mysterious, Pris is quite adept at manipulating men using her feminine charms, though if all else fails she can take them down with her superb hand-to-hand combat skills.

TRIVIA: *Pris's "date of inception" is Valentine's Day.*

Pygar

ORIGIN: Planet Lythion
SOURCE: *Barbarella* (1968)

This blind, beatific angel helps—and wins the heart of—the interstellar adventuress Barbarella during her mission to the planet Lythion in search of missing scientist Durand Durand.

QUOTE: *"An angel does not make love. An angel is love."*

Quark

ORIGIN: Planet Ferenginar
SOURCE: *Star Trek: Deep Space Nine* (TV series, 1993–1999)

The Ferengi bartender and unofficial minister of tourism aboard space station Deep Space Nine, Quark is forever working on some scheme designed to enhance his own financial position at the expense of others.

QUOTE: *"Never place friendship above profit."*

Qui-Gon

ORIGIN: Unknown
SOURCE: *Star Wars: The Phantom Menace* (1999)

Rangy Jedi Master Qui-Gon scores a daily double of influence in the Star Wars mythos: He both trains Obi-Wan Kenobi in the Jedi arts and recommends the young Anakin Skywalker (the future Darth Vader) for similar tutelage.

QUOTE: *"The ability to speak does not make you intelligent."*

SAREK

ORIGIN: Planet Vulcan
SOURCE: *Star Trek* (TV series, 1966–1969)

Vulcan diplomat, father of Spock, and an exemplar of the rigorous philosophy of absolute logic favored on his home world. Though he seems cold and analytical, Sarek is a deeply moral and spiritual being who often professes his love for his estranged son.
QUOTE: *"One does not thank logic."*

SHAD

ORIGIN: Planet Akir
SOURCE: *Battle Beyond the Stars* (1980)

Imbue your child with the spirit of pacifism by naming him (or her) after this peace-loving native of the planet Akir who must reluctantly round up a posse of seven samurai—oops, space cowboys—to liberate his planet from an evil despot in the magnificent B-movie space opera *Battle Beyond the Stars*.
QUOTE: *"No violent death is beautiful."*

SLARTIBARTFAST

ORIGIN: Planet Magrathea
SOURCE: *The Hitchhiker's Guide to the Galaxy* (BBC Radio, 1978)

Elderly Magrathean planet designer, awakened from a five-thousand-year sleep to work on the design of Earth Mark 2 after its destruction by the Vogons. A specialist in fjords, Slartibartfast is aggrieved when he is asked to design Africa instead of Norway.
QUOTE: *"Perhaps I'm old and tired, but I always think the chances of finding out what really is going on are so absurdly remote that the only thing to do is to say 'Hang the sense of it' and just keep yourself occupied."*

T'PAU

ORIGIN: Planet Vulcan
SOURCE: *Star Trek* (TV series, 1966–1969)

The name of this stern, eminent Vulcan matriarch is well known throughout the universe. Reportedly the only person ever to turn down a seat on the Federation Council, T'Pau spends her golden years officiating at Vulcan wedding ceremonies, including the abortive one for Mr. Spock.

TRON

ORIGIN: ENCOM Corporation computer
SOURCE: *Tron* (1982)

This pulsating geometric avatar exists only within the virtual reality video game milieu of the 1982 film *Tron*. A principled gladiator-hero who "fights for the users" in a computerized cosmos controlled by the sinister ENCOM Corporation, Tron teams up with his fellow avatars Clu and Yori to restore freedom to their cyberworld.
QUOTE: *"This code disc means freedom."*

TUVOK

ORIGIN: Planet Vulcan
SOURCE: *Star Trek: Voyager* (TV series, 1995–2001)

Tuvok is the Vulcan security and tactical officer aboard a starship stranded in the far-flung Delta Quadrant on *Star Trek: Voyager*. A full-blooded Vulcan, Tuvok nonetheless struggles to control his emotions at times, displaying flashes of a warrior mentality and chafing at the restraints of rigorous logic.
QUOTE: *"When every logical course of action is exhausted, the only option that remains is inaction."*

VASH

ORIGIN: 24th-century Earth
SOURCE: *Star Trek: The Next Generation* (TV series, 1987–1994)

Alluring female archaeologist with a shady secret agenda who serves as a recurring love interest for Captain Jean-Luc Picard on *Star Trek: The Next Generation*. Though beautiful, intelligent, and accomplished in her field, Vash does have an ethical blind spot when it comes to her *real* passion—collecting valuable artifacts from other planets.
QUOTE: "Even when I'm telling the truth no one believes me."

VIR

ORIGIN: Planet Centauri Prime
SOURCE: *Babylon 5* (TV series, 1994–1998)

Portly, timid Vir Cotto serves as the assistant to Centauri ambassador Londo Mollari on *Babylon 5*. The "black sheep" of a noble family, Vir is assigned to the space station at the behest of his relatives, who want him kept as far away as possible.

QUOTE: *"Every generation of Centauri mourns for the golden days when their power was like unto the gods. It's counterproductive. I mean, why make history if you fail to learn by it?"*

VISLOR

ORIGIN: Planet Trion
SOURCE: *Dr. Who* (BBC TV series, 1963–present)
Little-used first name of Vislor Turlough, a native of the planet Trion who travels with, and later betrays, the fifth incarnation of the Time Lord known as the Doctor. A squirrelly, shifty figure in dark blazer and skinny tie, Turlough poses as an ordinary British schoolboy but is actually a Trion exile in thrall to the evil Black Guardian.

QUOTE: *"What is it about Earth people that makes them think a futile gesture is a noble one?"*

VULTAN

ORIGIN: Planet Mongo
SOURCE: *Flash Gordon* (1980 film version)
Leader of the Hawkmen on the planet Mongo. Morbidly obese, with a booming basso profundo voice and an enormous Afro beard, Vultan leads his winged minions into an alliance with Flash Gordon in his fight against the evil Ming the Merciless. He is especially impressive when calling out orders mid-flight.

QUOTE: *"Hawkmen . . . DIIIIIIIVVVE!!!!"*

WORF

ORIGIN: Klingon Empire
SOURCE: *Star Trek: The Next Generation* (TV series, 1987–1994)
Worf serves as the tactical officer and security chief aboard the USS *Enterprise* on *Star Trek: The Next Generation*. A fierce Klingon warrior with a deeply ingrained sense of honor and loyalty, Worf is a reliable friend, loving father, and steadfast crewmate.

QUOTE: *"I am* not *a merry man!"*

YODA

ORIGIN: Unknown

SOURCE: *The Empire Strikes Back* (1980)

This diminutive Jedi master is a font of mystic wisdom as well as a demon with a lightsaber. His elfin aspect and unusual object-subject-verb speech pattern only add to his oracular power. The name Yoda may derive from the Sanskrit word *yoddha* meaning "warrior" or the Hebrew *yoddea*, or "one who knows."

QUOTE: *"Size matters not."*

YOR

ORIGIN: Post-apocalyptic Earth

SOURCE: *Yor, the Hunter from the Future* (1983)

Man's search for meaning lives on into its post-apocalyptic future thanks to Yor, the impeccably coiffed blond caveman hero of 1983's *Yor, the Hunter from the Future*. Not content to live in a world reduced to tribal primitivism in a nuclear holocaust, Yor sets out on a quest to discover the truth about his own past.

QUOTE: *"I'm Yor, the hunter. I come from the high mountains."*

YORI

ORIGIN: ENCOM Corporation computer

SOURCE: *Tron* (1982)

The digital avatar of a female ENCOM Corporation employee named Lora in the 1982 film *Tron*, Yori exists only inside the film's virtual reality video game milieu. She helps her fellow gladiators Clu and Tron defeat the evil Sark and restore freedom to their cyberworld.

QUOTE: *"I knew you'd escape. They haven't built a circuit that could hold you!"*

ZAPHOD

ORIGIN: A small planet in the vicinity of Betelgeuse

SOURCE: *The Hitchhiker's Guide to the Galaxy* (BBC Radio, 1978)

Two-headed, three-armed former president of the galaxy who now trolls the universe in a purloined spaceship in Douglas Adams's *The Hitchhiker's Guide to the Galaxy*. Among the eccentric, self-centered Zaphod's many accomplishments are inventing the Pan Galactic Gargle Blaster and being voted "Worst Dressed Sentient

Being in the Known Universe" seven years in a row.

QUOTE: *"I'll start with who, what, where, and when, followed by whither, whether, wherefore, and whence, and follow that up with a big side order of 'why.'"*

zardoz

ORIGIN: Post-apocalyptic Earth
SOURCE: *Zardoz* (1974)

Giant floating stone head, ruler of Earth's post-apocalyptic hinterlands in the 1974 sci-fi epic *Zardoz*. The name derives from a truncation of Wizard of Oz, the character on which this false deity was based. Also known as Mighty Zardoz.

QUOTE: *"The gun is good. The penis is evil. Go forth and kill!"*

zed

ORIGIN: Post-apocalyptic Earth
SOURCE: *Zardoz* (1974)

Exterminator-class "Brutal" who learns the truth about Zardoz, the giant stone head god who rules Earth's post-apocalyptic hinterlands in John Boorman's *Zardoz*. Hirsute and uncivilized, Zed is nonetheless a truth seeker at heart.

QUOTE: *"You stink of despair. Fight back! Fight for death, if that's what you want."*

zhora

ORIGIN: 21st-century Earth
SOURCE: *Blade Runner* (1982)

Beautiful and dangerous replicant assassin who works undercover as an exotic dancer in a future Los Angeles in which artificial life forms are hunted down and terminated. With her intimidating pet snake and imposing tattooed mien, Zhora presents a stiff challenge for the Blade Runner Deckard.

QUOTE: *"Do you think I'd be working in a place like this if I could afford a real snake?"*

CHAPTER 7

LAST NAMES FIRST

Some characters are so iconic they're only known by one name. No, we're not talking about Charo. We're talking about fictional characters whose first names are never given, or rarely used, so they become identified only by their last names. For a refreshing palate cleanser, here's a list of sci-fi character surnames that would work just as well— if not better—as first names.

Atoz

ORIGIN: Planet Sarpeidon
SOURCE: *Star Trek* (TV series, 1966–1969)

Instill a love of books in your child by naming it after this elderly librarian from the *Star Trek* episode "All Our Yesterdays," whose distinctive name derives from "A to Z." Mr. Atoz is the last surviving inhabitant of the planet Sarpeidon.

QUOTE: *"A library serves no purpose unless someone is using it."*

Benson

ORIGIN: Unknown
SOURCE: *Saturn 3* (1980)

Deranged, pill-popping pilot who terrorizes the two-person crew of an outer-space food research station in the 1980 film *Saturn 3*.

QUOTE: *"You have a great body. May I use it?"*

Brent

ORIGIN: 20th-century Earth
SOURCE: *Beneath the Planet of the Apes* (1970)

Like its counterparts Clint, Dirk, and Curt, the name Brent had its heyday in the machismo-fueled 1950s and 1960s. Perhaps that's why it was the preferred moniker of John Brent, the lantern-jawed, gravel-voiced astronaut in the 1970 feature *Beneath the Planet of the Apes*.

QUOTE: *"What the hell would I have to say to a gorilla?"*

Bryant

ORIGIN: 21st-century Earth
SOURCE: *Blade Runner* (1982)

The beleaguered captain of the Rep-Detect division of the LAPD in a future Los Angeles where artificial life forms known as replicants are hunted down and terminated, Bryant must persuade blade runner Rick Deckard to come out of retirement to take on one last mission.

QUOTE: *"I need ya, Deck. This is a bad one, the worst yet. I need the old blade runner. I need your magic."*

Case

ORIGIN: Future Earth
SOURCE: *Neuromancer* by William Gibson (published 1984)

Henry Dorsett Case is the drug-addicted hacker antihero of William Gibson's cyberpunk novel *Neuromancer*. Once a crack cyber-cowboy, lately gone to seed and in debt to multiple underworld figures, Case is motivated by a desire to reestablish his ability to "jack into the matrix"—the dizzying trove of computer data that is his real drug.

TRIVIA: *Gibson named this character after the "Case knife," a popular nineteenth-century pocketknife.*

Connor

ORIGIN: Earth, circa 1984
SOURCE: *The Terminator* (1984)

This handsome Irish name pays homage both to Sarah Connor, the strong-willed single mom who wages war with a relentless time-traveling cyborg, and, in future *Terminator* sequels, her son John Connor, who leads the entire human race in an apocalyptic war against the machines. (See also Sarah, p. 26.)

QUOTE: *"Come on. Do I look like the mother of the future? I'm not tough. I'm not organized. I can't even balance my checkbook!"*
VARIANTS: *Conner*

Granger

ORIGIN: Future Earth
SOURCE: *Fahrenheit 451* by Ray Bradbury (published 1953)

In Ray Bradbury's cautionary novel *Fahrenheit 451*, Granger is the leader of the "Book People," a wandering band of intellectually curious readers on a dystopian future Earth on which books are burned. A heroic figure dedicated to keeping the spirit of inquiry and imagination alive in the face of government oppression, Granger is a great name choice for the offspring of librarians, booksellers, and teachers.

QUOTE: *"I don't talk things, sir. I talk the meaning of things. I sit here and know I'm alive."*

HEPHAESTUS

ORIGIN: Unknown
SOURCE: *Battle Beyond the Stars* (1980)

In Greek mythology, Hephaestus is the god of the forge, a master of metallurgy disabled from birth. In the 1980 B-movie space opera *Battle Beyond the Stars*, the brilliant but eccentric Dr. Hephaestus is more than merely lame; he's permanently soldered to a nourishing computer core and serviced in his every need by a retinue of singing androids aboard a floating research station.

QUOTE: *"Forms must prey on other forms."*

KANE

ORIGIN: 22nd-century Earth
SOURCE: *Alien* (1979)

Executive officer aboard the commercial towing vessel *Nostromo* in the sci-fi classic *Alien*, famous principally for his grisly demise, in which an acid-blooded alien incubus bursts from his stomach, sending gore and entrails flying. Possibly a name to avoid unless you're steering your child toward a career in gastroenterology.

QUOTE: *"Ahhhhhhhh!"*

KIRK

ORIGIN: 23rd-century Earth
SOURCE: *Star Trek* (TV series, 1966–1969)

An Old Norse word meaning "church," Kirk is also the surname of the finest captain in Starfleet, James Tiberius Kirk of the USS *Enterprise*. Dashing and impulsive, with a roving eye for the ladies (of any species), Kirk is dedicated to the safety of his ship and crew, a decisive leader with a strong sense of duty.

QUOTE: *"I'm from Iowa. I just work in outer space."*
VARIANTS: *Kerk, Kirke*

LEELA

ORIGIN: 30th-century Earth
SOURCE: *Futurama* (TV series, 1999–2003)

Turanga Leela, better known simply as Leela, is the on-again, off-again love interest of Philip J. Fry on the TV sci-fi animated series *Futurama*. A one-eyed mutant of unknown parentage, Leela overcame her lack of depth perception to become a ship's pilot for Planet Express. Her full name is a reference to the *Turangalîla-*

Symphonie by Olivier Messianen.

QUOTE: *"At the risk of sounding negative, no."*

OTHER NOTABLE SCI-FI LEELAS: *Leela (*Dr. Who *warrior companion)*

LOGAN

ORIGIN: 20th-century Earth

SOURCE: *The Incredible Hulk* #180 (Marvel Comics, 1974)

Name adopted by James Howlett III, scion of a wealthy Canadian family, to honor his birth father, Thomas Logan, the humble groundskeeper on his family's estate. The mutant Logan is better known by his nickname, Wolverine. A member of the X-Men, he is gifted from birth with an impregnable adamantium skeleton, retractable razor-sharp claws, and superhuman senses. While often taken for a dumb brute, Logan is in fact a complex, cosmopolitan man who has mastered numerous languages and martial arts.

QUOTE: *"Why is every other word out of someone's mouth to me animal?"*

MORBIUS

ORIGIN: Planet Altair 4

SOURCE: *Forbidden Planet* (1956)

Brilliant scientist Dr. Edward Morbius lives with his beautiful daughter and robot servant in an artificial utopia created by the ancient race called the Krell on the planet Altair 4. Even with an IQ nearly doubled by the miraculous Krell "educator" machine, Morbius remains a prisoner of his own subconscious—unwittingly directing a series of attacks against a crew of space travelers who come to rescue him.

QUOTE: *"My evil self is at the door, and I have no power to stop it."*

MORDEN

ORIGIN: Unknown

SOURCE: *Babylon 5* (TV series, 1994–1998)

Mysterious, vaguely sinister human emissary of the Shadows on the TV series *Babylon 5*. While exceedingly courteous and polite, Mr. Morden nonetheless cuts a menacing figure and seems to be harboring a hidden agenda.

QUOTE: *"Flesh is transitory, flesh is a prison, flesh is . . . an instrument. Flesh can be replaced. And flesh does as it's told."*

MXYZPTLK

ORIGIN: Fifth Dimension
SOURCE: *Superman* #30 (1944)

Adventurous parents seeking a truly distinctive name for their child would do well to consider this all-but-unpronounceable moniker honoring impish Superman villain Mr. Mxyzptlk. A clown-ish irritant from the Fifth Dimension, Mxyzptlk befuddles Superman on numerous occasions with his magic tricks and pranks. Want to get rid of him? Say his name backward and send him back to the Fifth Dimension.

QUOTE: *"I am no ordinary man. I am Mr. Mxyzptlk!"*

NADA

ORIGIN: 20th-century Earth
SOURCE: *They Live* (1988)

Unemployed drifter John Nada gets a whole new outlook on life after he dons a pair of mysterious sunglasses that allow him to detect Earth's infiltration by a race of scabrous, skull-faced aliens in the 1988 sci-fi chiller *They Live*.

QUOTE: *"I have come here to chew bubblegum and kick ass. And I'm all out of bubblegum."*

TAKO

ORIGIN: 20th-century Earth
SOURCE: *King Kong vs. Godzilla* (1962)

Japanese pharmaceutical company executive Mr. Tako dispatches two of his employees to Pharoh Island to search for medicinal berries in the 1962 monster fest *King Kong vs. Godzilla*. Instead they run smack into the revived giant ape and eventually his fire-breathing lizard rival.

TRIVIA: Tako *means "octopus" in Japanese—an apparent reference to the giant octopus Kong battles in the film.*

TAYLOR

ORIGIN: 20th-century Earth
SOURCE: *Planet of the Apes* (1968)

Misanthropic spaceship commander (first name George), the so-called golden boy of the class of '72, who finds himself stranded on a post-apocalyptic Earth ruled by simians in *Planet of the Apes*. Taylor's cynical view of the universe is validated when he is whipped, bound, gagged, and nearly castrated by his ape captors.

QUOTE: *"I can't help thinking somewhere in the universe there has to be something better than man."*

VARIANTS: *Tailer, Tailor, Tayler*

Trent

ORIGIN: 20th-century Earth
SOURCE: *Plan 9 from Outer Space* (1959)

The spirit of resistance to alien domination lives when you name your child after Jeff Trent, the dim but defiant airline-pilot hero of the 1959 sci-fi zombie classic *Plan 9 from Outer Space*. Luckily for Earth, his home abuts a graveyard, putting this half-cocked pistol of a man on the front lines of defense against invasion, using resurrected corpses as shock troops.

QUOTE: *"I'll tell you one thing, if a little green man pops out at me, I'm shooting first and asking questions later."*

Wash

ORIGIN: Unknown
SOURCE: *Firefly* (TV series, 2002)

Hoban "Wash" Washburne is the easygoing pilot of the transport ship *Serenity* on TV's *Firefly*. Laid-back and well-liked, Wash exhibits a dry sense of humor, which he often uses to defuse conflicts among his crewmates. He has a fondness for toy dinosaurs.

QUOTE: *"Sleepiness is weakness of character. Ask anyone."*

Wolff

ORIGIN: 20th-century Earth
SOURCE: *Spacehunter: Adventures in the Forbidden Zone* (1983)

Jaded intergalactic bounty hunter who treks to a junkyard planet to rescue three stranded Earth women with some help from an excitable teenage moppet in the 1983 space opera *Spacehunter: Adventures in the Forbidden Zone*.

QUOTE: *"If you think our deal is for me to babysit you for the next two hundred years, you're dreaming. I don't remember us saying anything about adoption!"*

INDEX BY NAME

Where names apply to both sexes, XY = male and XX = female.